D.J.'s WORST ENEMY

Also by ROBERT BURCH

A FUNNY PLACE TO LIVE
TYLER, WILKIN, AND SKEE
SKINNY

D.J.'s WORST ENEMY

by ROBERT BURCH

ILLUSTRATED BY
EMIL WEISS

THE VIKING PRESS NEW YORK

Printed in the U. S. A. by The Vail-Ballou Press, Inc.

For my sister, Emily Scovill,
her husband, Tom, and their family:
Tommy, Sally, Russell, and Joan

CONTENTS

D.J.'s
WORST
ENEMY

I

THE BULL IN THE THICKET

We were down in the pasture seeing if either one of us could walk across the foot log on our hands. Nutty gave it a try and I sat on the bank and talked about what we ought to be doing. "Let's wander over to the Castor place," I said. "If we don't go over there and stir up a little trouble, they're gonna think we're scared of 'em."

"We *are* scared of 'em," said Nutty, which shows how nutty Nutty really is.

"Just because they licked us the last time doesn't mean we're scared," I insisted. "It merely means we haven't found it convenient lately to get ourselves over there."

Nutty lost his balance and fell in the shallow water about midstream. "If they want to fight," he argued, "let them pay us a visit. It ain't a step farther for them to walk from over there to over here than it is for us to walk from over here to over there."

"Yes, it is," I said. "It's downhill for us. And besides, we're the ones hankering to fight. They're plumb peace-loving." I got up to leave.

"It's uphill coming back," said Nutty, wading out of the water.

"Aw, come on! After we whip a few Castors, it'll take an uphill pull just to get us simmered down again."

He climbed back on the log and tried to cross it by hopping on one foot, but slid off after two hops. He landed at the edge of the stream, miring up in mud to his ankles. "All right, let's go," he said, just as we heard the creak of the pasture gate being opened.

I'd been supposed to grease the hinges on the gate for a month or more, but had kept putting it off. I'd do it when Pa got around to notifying me that he was telling me once and for all to get it done. In the meantime, it was convenient for me and Nutty that it made those loud scraping noises. It warned us when anybody was around, which came in handy if we happened to be smoking rabbit tobacco, a weed that grows hereabouts, or doing anything else we didn't choose to be caught at.

Anyway, just as Nutty was agreeing that we would go over to the Castors, the gate sounded clear and loud.

"That's Clara May with the buttermilk," I said, without going to the edge of the thicket to look out. Clara May's my sister. She's a year older than I am.

"How you know it's her?"

" 'Cause today's churning has been done already," I explained, "and somebody has to put the milk in the spring. How else would it keep cool?" I went on to tell that I was supposed to have brought it myself after lunch.

Nutty laughed. "How'd you get away without being caught?"

"I eased away from the table while Mamma was trying to convince Skinny Little Renfroe he ought to eat another biscuit and gravy to keep his strength up. At the same time she was arguing with Clara May that thirteen ain't old enough to have a permanent wave."

Nutty walked out to the edge of the bushes and peeked toward the open pasture, then said over his shoulder, "Hey, D.J. It's Clara May with the buttermilk," as if I hadn't said exactly the same thing the minute before.

"Let's pull our trick on them again," I suggested.

13

"Renfroe ain't with her," said Nutty, and I thought this was strange. Skinny Little Renfroe is my five-and-a-half-year-old brother, and whenever he's not trailing around after me, he's automatically tagging along with Clara May.

"Then let's trick her by herself," I said.

"She won't be fooled again."

"Sure she will," I said. "Clara May ain't got no sense."

The trick we had in mind was the one we had sprung on them yesterday. We'd hidden behind a tree near the path that ran through the thicket. And when Clara May and Skinny Little Renfroe came poking along on their way to the spring, we snorted and bellowed like Pa's Jersey bull. They struck out running and didn't stop till they got back to the gate.

Nutty agreed that we'd try it again, and we picked a spot, a different one this time, and waited. It would take both of us to do a proper imitation of the bull. We had practiced it last week till we got it down perfect. Nutty did the low moo sound and then I'd come in on the snorting, or bellowing part. Between us, we sounded every bit as terrifying as Pa's bull, and that's awful terrifying.

Actually, the bull is supposed to stay down in the lot near the barn, but he jumps the fence about half the time and ambles around the pasture. And when he gets tired of snorting and pawing up the ground trying to impress the cows, there ain't nothing he had rather do than chase children. I'm not necessarily afraid of him, but it's the way Pa says: you have to use judgment when dealing with a mean Jersey bull. They've been known to kill folks.

We kept still, waiting for Clara May. Her footsteps were coming closer when suddenly behind us there was a low mooing sound, followed by a wild bellowing. There wasn't but one thing it could be, and nobody had to tell me and Nutty that we'd better light out of there in a hurry. We almost knocked the buttermilk jars out of Clara May's hands as we flew past her. "Come on," I called. "Drop the milk and run! The bull's in there!"

Nutty and I didn't stop till we were at the gate. Then we looked back and saw Clara May standing near the thicket. She motioned for us to come back, pointing down below the barn.

"What's she pointing at?" I asked, looking in that direction.

"The bull, I reckon," answered Nutty. "There he is grazing inside the lot."

"How can that be?" I asked, "when you know as well as I do that he just then ran us out of the thicket."

"I thought so, too," said Nutty, "but that's him down yonder for sure."

"Then somebody else's bull must be in the thicket. We better go warn Clara May. She's so crazy she'll go on walking in there."

When we got back to where she was standing, we told her she'd better leave off going to the spring, but she wouldn't believe us about it being dangerous. She said, "We've got the only bull in this end of the county, you know that," and went walking ahead along the path.

We eased along after her. I'd tell her one minute to be careful and the next minute that I didn't care if she did get chased. At the same time, I peered about for any sign of a bull.

When we got to the spring, there sat Skinny Little Renfroe on one of the big rocks back of it. He was having a drink of water from the gourd we use as a dipper. I asked, "How'd you get in here?"

"Just walked in," he answered.

Clara May asked, in her sassy voice, "How'd you think he got here—by aeroplane?" Then she said, "Hop down from there, Renfroe, and help me get this milk fixed." She never called him Skinny Little Renfroe the way I did. The only reason I called him that was to make him mad. I thought maybe if he got sick of hearing himself called such a name, he'd stop following me around.

The two of them leaned over the spring to put the jars of milk in the water. While they were doing it,

Skinny Little Renfroe snickered. Then Clara May did, and then he did again. Finally they were giggling.

There's not a thing funny about putting buttermilk in a spring of cold water. First, you see that the jars are closed tight, so none of the milk will seep out. Then you feel around in the sand at the bottom to find a level spot to rest them on, and that's all there is to it. There's nothing funny about it, but Clara May and Skinny Little Renfroe giggled so much they almost never got those two jars settled. They eventually succeeded, then stood up.

"What's so funny?" I asked, and that struck them as a good joke. They laughed in a hysterical fashion. Every now and then they slowed down and one or the other would start to say something, but they'd be off again on a giggling spell before any words came out.

It's disgusting to watch Clara May laughing so hard that tears come to her eyes. And when Skinny Little Renfroe laughs, he's plumb comical-looking. He's got a thin little pinched-in face full of freckles, and ears that have outdistanced the rest of his growth. He's not prize-looking at best, but when he laughs, and especially if you're not busy laughing at the same time, you can't help but be struck by the sight. It seems that all you see is a mouth full of teeth with a big ear at each end of it.

Nutty and I sat there, watching those two make fools of themselves until they got tired of laughing and sat down to rest. In a few minutes, Clara May got up and reached over and dipped herself a gourdful of water. Then she filled it again and asked Skinny Little Renfroe if he wanted a drink.

"I'll take another sip," he answered, accepting the gourd. After he'd drunk all he wanted and emptied what was left onto the weeds back of him, he stood up.

Clara May said, "Renfroe, before we leave I'd like to hear you do one of your imitations. D. J. and Nutty might like it too."

I groaned, not feeling up to listening to him make some of his silly sounds, telling us it was a galloping horse, or a blue jay having a fight, or a cat in the fig bushes, or whatever.

But Nutty was just stupid enough to say, "Yeah, let's hear one of your imitations."

Skinny Little Renfroe's face lit up. He was all the time doing his imitations but I didn't recall that anybody had ever requested one. Even Clara May got tired of them and I couldn't figure out what had gotten into her that she brought up the subject now. Skinny Little Renfroe stood up straight and asked, "Would you like to hear a coon dog barking up a sweet gum tree at a possum in the moonlight?" Pointing toward a big tree, he asked, "Is that a sweet gum?"

I told him that it was a water oak, but he walked over and stood by it, anyway. Talking mostly to Nutty, he explained, "Now you have to imagine that I'm a coon dog and that there's a possum up in this sweet gum tree."

"I told you it was a water oak," I said.

Ignoring me, he said to Nutty, "You have to imagine that this water oak is a sweet gum tree and that I'm a coon dog and there's a possum up—"

Clara May interrupted him this time. "Renfroe," she said, "you're not doing the right imitation. You know the one I was talking about—your newest one."

He nodded. "I know, but Nutty wants so bad to hear them, I think I'll do several of the others first."

"We'll be here all day if you do," said Clara May. "Hurry it up and let's go out to the mailbox. Maybe *you-know-what* will get here today."

The *you-know-what* was aimed at me. It was something the two of them had ordered with the money Clara May earned earlier in the season. After we had helped Pa get our own crops in good shape, she and I had hired out to chop cotton for neighboring farmers who needed extra help.

We had made pretty good wages and I spent mine on things I wanted for myself. But Clara May had divided her money with Skinny Little Renfroe on account of he's not big enough yet to earn any of his own. Then she talked him into putting his half of the money back with her half and them ordering something together. That's how crazy she is.

They wouldn't tell me what they had ordered because they said I was indifferent and never would go in with them on anything. But I didn't care and wasn't at all curious—except that it could turn out to be something nice.

The mention of the *you-know-what* and that it might this very minute be up at the crossroads in our mailbox was enough to change the performance. Skinny Little Renfroe skipped over the coon dog and the possum and got on with the imitation Clara May wanted him to do. He took a step away from the tree, adjusted his feet, cleared his throat twice, and announced: "An imitation. By Renfroe Madison." Then he leaned his head down and gave a low moo, followed by a loud bellow. When he got to the tail-end he leaned his head back on the snorting part and sounded for all the world like Pa's bull on the rampage. It was disgusting. Next, he pawed the ground with his right foot and laughed to beat the band. Clara May laughed too.

I got up to leave without saying anything, but Nutty, stupid Nutty, asked, "How'd you slip in to scare us without making any noise?"

"I climbed over the gate so you wouldn't hear it opening."

Clara May said, "And as soon as he got into the thicket, I came through the gate and screeched it good and loud so you'd know I was on the way." Looking at me, she added, "We knew if you were anywhere around you'd try to scare me again, the way you always run a joke in the ground."

The two of them started out the path toward the trail that led to the mailbox, laughing until they were out of hearing distance.

Nutty and I sat down by the spring and I stared into the water. The afternoon was ruined. It's not that I can't take a joke, but it was humiliating to think that dumb Skinny Little Renfroe by himself could sound more like Pa's bull than Nutty and me put together. I didn't even feel up to going over to the Castors to pick a fight. That would just have to wait until another time.

2

"TOO MANY FROGS ON ONE CREEK BANK"

Pa sent me out before breakfast the next morning to try to catch the mules. We hadn't worked either one of them in a week or more and I knew Twilight would have gone wild. Effie is gentle, no matter what, but give Twilight a few days without putting a bridle on her and you'd think she never had seen one before.

This time she stopped her grazing and stood and watched me get closer to her. "Whoa, Girl," I kept saying. "Steady there now." But when I was no more than two feet away, she turned and ran off—just far enough for me to have to start over. She kept doing the same thing until I decided to go ahead and catch Effie, who was waiting patiently in the shade of a big poplar.

Twilight followed after me, but I pretended to ignore her while I talked to Effie. "We may not let Twilight come with us," I said. "Makes no difference if it does take more than one mule to pull a two-horse wagon." I put a bridle on Effie and led her off. Twilight followed us every step of the way across the pasture and into the barn. I closed the door quickly and had outfoxed her for sure, but, of course, next time she might get the best of me. You never can tell about mules.

After we ate, Clara May and I picked a basket of squash and one of cucumbers, and all the tomatoes we could find. Pa would take them along to neighbor-out with some of the folks up the road.

He said, "I'd better return Ol' Man Cato's guano distributor at the same time," and I pushed it across the yard and helped lift it onto the wagon. Then I brought out the mules and we hitched them up.

Andrew Jackson, our old black-and-tan hound, came ambling across the yard and hopped over the tailgate. It's the only time he ever exerts any energy. When the wagon is being hitched up for a trip, he always stirs himself to get aboard. Other than that, he's got no ambition at all. But he does love to ride in the wagon and the chances of it pulling out of the yard without him are unlikely. His luck runs better than mine. I asked Pa, "Can't I go into town with you?"

"Not this time," he said, which is what I expected him to say. He began mapping out chores he wanted me to do while he was gone. "See about the drainage ditch first," he said. "Those weeds are clogging it up and the water'll run off wrong next time it rains if something's not done."

"What's the use in laying-by," I complained, "if it don't give us time to do something besides work?" Laying-by is what folks around here call the time between the last cultivating of our crops, cotton and corn mostly, and the time to harvest them. Whenever we finish the weeding and hoeing, we say we're "out of the grass," and whenever we're "out of the grass" we consider ourselves laid-by. It's all the same thing.

Pa said, "Now D. J.! The work on a farm doesn't ever get completely laid-by, you know that." Then he added, "And after you clean out the ditch, get in the corncrib and see if you can shuck enough corn to take to the mill tomorrow." I perked up at that. Not that I like shucking corn all that much, but a trip to the mill is something special.

"Can I go to the mill with you?" I asked.

"Why not?" said Pa, as he cracked the whip to get

the mules started. "Our crops are laid-by, aren't they?"
It's as hard to figure out Pa as it is Twilight.

I went first and chopped out the weeds that were
growing in the drainage ditch and then got started in
the corncrib. Skinny Little Renfroe was busy in the
fig bushes just outside it. It was his job to get to the figs
as soon as they ripened—and ahead of the birds. Blue
jays were fussing on a pecan limb overhead when I'd
gone into the crib and a few minutes later were making
so much noise that I went out to try to quiet them.
But I found that they had flown away and the noise
was being made by Skinny Little Renfroe imitating
them.

"Were you looking for the jay birds?" he asked.

"I knew it was you," I said. "Can't you pick figs
without making all that racket?"

"That wasn't a racket," he said. "It was an imitation.
I can do it some more if you want to hear it."

I didn't even bother to answer, but went back to
work. And he went on with his imitations. First he'd
pretend to be the blue jays squawking, then he'd be
himself and pretend to be shooing them off. "Go on, I
tell you! Get out!" he would yell, making a whooshing
noise next that was supposed to be the birds flying
away. Then he would get busy, scurrying about so fast
that the handle of his bucket practically sang as it was
swung around. When he tired of bird imitations, he

switched over to trying to copy the squeaking sound of the bucket handle.

Eventually he had picked, or eaten, all the figs that were ripe and stepped over to the corncrib. He stood in the door and asked, "Want to hear me imitate the bull again?" At that, he gave a low moo and then the bellow.

Mamma called from the back porch. "Renfroe, come back to the house or get in the feed room with D. J. It sounds as if the bull's out again."

I answered, "That was Skinny Little Renfroe. The bull's in the lot."

Mamma yelled back, "Now, Renfroe, don't scare me like that. It gives me heart failure."

"All right," he answered happily. "I won't do it any more." Then he called to Clara May, who was hanging out the wash, "Reckon *you-know-what* will get here today?"

"Just might," she called back. "Never can tell what'll come in the mail."

Then he hopped over in the crib. "I can't tell you what we've ordered off after," he said, as if I had asked him, "but I'll help you shuck the corn."

"Get that basket," I directed, "and fish around in this pile of nubbins. Most of them are too small to be of any account, but when you come across one that feels heavy enough, shuck it and throw it in the corner."

He started right in as if he were powerfully interested in helping me, but after he had shucked four or five ears, he suddenly had a matter to discuss. "Since I'm helping out," he said, "I guess I'll get to go to the mill tomorrow too. Be sure and tell Pa that me and you *together* did the work. All right?"

"Just get on out of here," I said, "if that's how come you're helping."

"Too late now," he said. "I've already started."

"How'd you know about the trip to the mill, anyway?"

"I heard Pa telling you this morning," he explained. "I was sitting back of the pomegranate bush."

"What were you doing there?"

"Listening to you and Pa talk. Would you like to hear me imitate a cat bird trying to scare a squirrel away from a peach that fell on the ground during a high wind and is gonna be eaten up by a terrapin right under their noses if they don't watch out?"

"No, I would not," I said firmly, and I lit into lecturing to him on what a pest he was. But it didn't bother him a bit. He never could bring himself to realize that anybody ever meant anything except something nice.

Ten minutes later, Nutty came along. "I thought you were coming over early," I said. He lives with his grandparents, and since his grandpa is a retired man who used to work for the railroad, they don't try to do too much farming. That's why Nutty usually has more free time than the rest of us.

"I had to stake tomatoes before I could get away," he said. "What all have you got to do?"

"I've finished everything but shucking the corn."

He volunteered to help and climbed over into the feed room. "Howdy-do there, Renfroe," he said. "Been scaring anybody lately with your bull number?"

"Just Mamma. I promised not to do it again, but I've thought up a new one. Want to hear it?"

"It's what I came for," said Nutty, turning a bucket wrong-side up and sitting down on it. He grabbed up some of the corn and went straight to work.

Skinny Little Renfroe acted as if he thought Nutty meant what he had said. He got to his feet to perform. "Well, this one's about two frogs sitting on a creek bank," he explained. "One of 'em is an old frog—that'll be the deep croaking. And the high-pitched sound will be a young one who hasn't been too long turned from a tadpole. In fact, this is probably his first time sitting on the bank."

"You don't have to tell us anybody's life story," I said. Turning to Nutty, I added, "That reminds me, let's go frog-gigging one night before long."

Skinny Little Renfroe said excitedly, "Let's do."

"I wasn't talking to you," I said, and went ahead discussing it with Nutty.

"Too Many Frogs on One Creek Bank"

Skinny Little Renfroe said, "I didn't finish telling you about the frogs."

Nutty turned back to him. "We want to hear all about them."

"If you listen close, you'll hear them jump in the water at the very end. The loud ker-plop will be—"

I interrupted him. "We know. The loud ker-plop will be the big frog hitting the water and the high-pitched ker-plop will be the one who can't get over the fact that he ain't still a tadpole. Do it and then get out of here. Nutty and I have things to discuss."

He cleared his throat and announced: "An imitation. By Renfroe Madison." Then he began the croaking. Twenty frogs couldn't have stirred up as much fuss. He kept on and on, first in a deep voice, then in a shrill one, then back to the deep one. He was whirling his arms at the same time. I don't know what that was supposed to signify and doubt if he did. It was funny at first, but he carried on too long and finally I tossed a light ear of corn, shuck and all, at him. It slowed him down a little and he tapered off on the croaking till the big frog jumped in. After the ker-plop of it landing in the water, the little frog, sounding more like a sparrow chirping than a frog, continued to croak until a high-pitched ker-plop landed it in the water.

"It took long enough," I said, and Nutty clapped his hands as if he had seen a circus.

29

Skinny Little Renfroe drew a deep breath and started croaking again, louder than ever.

"Hey, wait a minute!" I yelled. "You've finished."

He interrupted his croaking long enough to say hurriedly, "The big frog's done crawled onto the bank again," and went right ahead with the noise. It's likely he'd be at it till yet if Nutty hadn't said, "I believe maybe there are too many frogs on one creek bank. But it was a good imitation, all right."

I told Skinny Little Renfroe, "Now you go on off. We've got things to talk about."

But he sat down. "You can talk, I don't mind listening."

"*We* mind," I said, trying to sound gruff. It's the only way he will pay any attention to what's said to him.

"I think I'll just stay on with you," he said, at the same time getting to his feet.

"No, you won't!" I said, and I picked up another ear of corn and threw it at him. I knew when it left my hand that I had misgauged the size of it. In the shucks, you can't always tell a heavy ear of corn from a light nubbin. And I'd grabbed one in a hurry from a pile that was mostly nubbins. But it turned out to be a heavy ear. And on top of that, I'd thrown it with more force than I meant to.

It hit Skinny Little Renfroe on the ankle. He jumped

in the air about two feet and when he landed on the foot that had been hit, his leg almost buckled under him. Then he jumped up and down on his other foot. He stopped for just a second and bent over his ankle, holding onto it with his hands. He didn't say anything, but he looked at me as if I had dealt him his death blow. Then he jumped out of the crib and went hobbling off toward the house.

I noticed blood on the sill where he'd crossed it and I saw that he was bleeding as he went along. I leaped over the sill and ran after him. When I caught up, I tried to put one arm around his shoulders; he could lean on me and not have to put all his weight on the foot that had been hit. But he pushed me away. "You didn't have to throw at me," he said, sort of sniffing. "I was getting up to leave." It was a lie, of course, because he never left anywhere till he was run off. But I hadn't meant to hurt him; that was a mean thing for me to do.

Mamma came out on the porch and I knew automatically to run fetch the can of kerosene. It's what we use whenever any of us are injured. I brought it quickly and Mamma sloshed it onto the wound, a larger patch of broken skin than I'd realized. "This will help take the soreness out," she said, telling me next, "Now run to the rag bag and bring a clean, white cloth."

31

I was back in a minute with an outgrown nightshirt that had been washed and saved for such purposes as this.

When the bleeding had almost stopped, the bruise was beginning to turn bluish-black. Mamma said, "Now tell me how it happened," talking to Skinny Little Renfroe instead of me.

He didn't answer for a few seconds, then he said, "I hit it on something in the corncrib. I was jumping up to leave."

"Well, you must watch where you jump from now on," she warned, without asking any other questions. She was more concerned about easing his pain than in knowing exactly what had happened.

While she continued to dab at the wound with the cloth soaked in kerosene, Skinny Little Renfroe looked up at me and smiled. I figured it was his way of saying that he hadn't told on me. He kept looking up at me for some sign that I understood, but I turned and walked off without looking back.

Partway across the yard, I stopped. Maybe I ought to return to the house. If I wasn't going to thank Skinny Little Renfroe for not telling on me, I could at least let him know that I realized he hadn't. But instead, I started once more toward the crib.

Just then, a blue jay flew into the fig bushes and landed on one of the top limbs. It squawked loudly, as if to announce to all its friends that the boy who had shooed them out was no longer there. It made me mad. Maybe I was really madder at myself than anything else; but whatever, I picked up a stone, took careful aim, and threw it with all my strength. An instant later the bird toppled from the limb to the ground, where it fluttered its wings and shivered. Soon it was dead.

3

TROUBLE-MAKING

In the afternoon I convinced Nutty that we absolutely had to get ourselves over to the Castors.

"Me and you could just wrestle for a while," he said, "and save ourselves a long walk."

"Wrestling for fun and fighting are two different things," I said. "Come on, let's get going." He still

34

didn't take to the idea, but he came along, anyway.

We took a short cut through the woods, touching onto Flint River for a part of the way. Fishing poles that we knew belonged to the Castors had been stuck into the bank to hold them in place. The lines dangled in the water. "Let's steal their set hooks," I suggested, pulling the first bamboo pole out of the clay that held it.

"We ought not to steal them," said Nutty, "but I guess we could hide one or two and make them have to look for 'em." But I had a better idea. Instead of hiding the poles, we'd put something on all the hooks. Then when the Castors came along, they'd think they'd caught a lot of fish until they saw it was a trick. It took a little while to load the hooks, mostly with pine cones and sticks and clumps of fern that grew at the water's edge. We also found a dead crow and put it on one of the hooks. That would be the best joke of all. Then we cut through a cornfield and made our way to the Castors' yard.

All four of the boys were across on the other side of the house, beyond the woodpile. To get to them, we had to walk past Doris, their sister, who was on this side of the yard doing the family washing. She was in our grade at school and we didn't like her at all. In fact, I think it was on account of her that we were always picking fights with her brothers. Not that they were responsible for her acting the way she did—talking snippy and all that. But we couldn't hit her, so we sort of took out our aggravation on them. At least, that might have been part of it. She was the only girl in their family, except two little bitty ones, and they were most of the time inside with their mother or crawling around the back steps and not in anybody's way.

Doris was chunking up the fire under the washpots when we came near. She took her long stirring paddle next and poked about in the soapy water in one of the pots. We didn't say "howdy" or anything, and she pretended not to see us. With the stick she lifted a bed sheet out of the soapy water and dumped it into the rinsing pot. Then when we were even with her, she propped herself against the paddle and said, "I just can't wait for school to start so's I can tell everybody about my brothers giving you all such a licking. And every one of 'em younger than you!"

I had planned not to say anything to her, but that's the way she is. She always says something smarty that's got to be answered back if you have any self-respect. "Well, you just hang around this time," I told her.

Instead of answering me, she called to her brothers, who were stacking cordwood. "You all come on up here. Here are Nutty and D. J. presenting themselves before us."

We walked on out to where the boys were. Monroe

was the oldest. He was a year younger than me and Nutty but was about our size. "Howdy," he said, smiling as if he thought we were paying a friendly visit. "We ain't seen you all in a long time."

"Been busy," I said, cutting him short. "We've had more important things on our mind."

"Sit down and tell us about 'em," said Britt, the next-oldest, motioning toward a log nearby as if it were a parlor bench. Nutty started to sit down but I gave him a cross look and he stayed where he was.

"We ain't here to be sociable," I said. "We've come to whip every one of you."

"Aw, it's too hot to fight," said Monroe.

"No, it ain't," called Doris, from over by the wash-pots. "You all go ahead and run our company off. I'm tired of looking at them."

Chester told me, "Don't pay any attention to her. She don't like you all very much."

I said good and loud, so she'd be certain to hear, "We don't like her either."

Doris said, "I can't remember us inviting anybody to come a-calling this afternoon."

The boys ignored her, and Hoot, the youngest one, told us, "We've got a watermelon cooling in the barrel by the well."

"Say, you have!" said Nutty.

Britt said, "There'll be enough for all of us if you'd like some."

"Of course we would!" said Nutty, but I didn't agree.

"Why, we're plumb sick of watermelon," I told them. "Why, I expect we've already eaten more watermelons this week than any of you are apt to see in your lifetime." It sounded even more impressive than I'd thought it would. It took Nutty by surprise, naturally, since we'd discussed on the way over how anxious we were for one of Pa's melons to go on and get ripe. I thought for a minute he was going to desert me and team up with the Castors. I'd better do something quick. Chester was nearest to me so I reached out and pushed him off balance.

"You stop that," said Monroe. "He ain't big as you are."

"You ain't neither," I told him. "But there's four of you."

"Five, if I'm needed," called Doris to her brothers. "Go ahead and beat up D. J. You needn't whip Nutty if you're not a-mind to. He ain't the trouble-maker."

"Nutty's in this with me," I yelled, as much to keep him reminded of it as anything else.

Chester had gotten up from where I'd pushed him. "Then let's fight," he said, and he started wrestling me, but Nutty pulled him off. Then he and Nutty and Britt were at it, and I started in on Monroe—and I realized at once that it was a mistake. Monroe wasn't but eleven and I was twelve, but he sure had grown

38

lately. I finally threw him to the ground, but he rolled over on me a second later. We wrestled around, ripping and snorting, and once when I was on top, Hoot started to pull me off. But Monroe told him he could handle me by himself.

Before long, Nutty and Britt and Chester had stopped fighting and were standing around watching us as if they'd purchased tickets. I called out, "What's ailing the rest of you?"

Nutty said, "We called a truce."

About then Monroe scrambled out from under me and a minute later had me down. Chester felt called on to finish explaining why they weren't fighting. "We licked Nutty," he said, and reached out and patted him on the back, all of them grinning like good pals.

Monroe and I went on wrestling and I had one of his elbows back of him when he managed to break the hold. By then, we were both pretty near worn out, but he pinned my shoulders to the ground and counted ten. "Give up?" he asked.

Hoot, who hadn't contributed anything to the fight except to be brushed aside, said, "He don't have to give up if you hold his shoulders to the ground whilst you count ten."

Monroe didn't pay any attention and asked again, "Give up?"

"Yeah," I said eventually, "I give up." But he went right on holding me down.

"How come you don't let him go?" asked Nutty. "He said he gave up."

Chester, feeling compelled as always to explain things, said, " 'Cause D. J.'s word is not any good. He's liable to get up and start fighting again."

Doris was standing over us now with that long paddle. "Let him go," she said. "If he goes back on his word, I'll knock him in the head with this."

Monroe said to me, "No more fighting till next time, all right?"

"All right," I agreed, and he let me up. If I was planning to do any of my cheating tricks like saying I had my fingers crossed all the time and start back to fighting, I changed my mind quick. Doris was holding that washpot paddle like a baseball bat and I knew she would welcome an excuse to swat me with it.

I took plenty of time to brush myself off and was trying to think up something to say that would be insulting enough to include everybody when we saw a wagon coming along the road. It was Pa, returning from his trip to town. He was letting Twilight and Effie move along at a pretty good trot and was soon close by. "Whoa!" he called to the mules, stopping to speak to us.

Everybody said "Howdy" except Hoot, and he said, "Where you been at, Mr. Madison?" I never have known an eight-year-old to be so nosy.

Doris said, "Don't say 'Where you been at?' Say 'Where have you been?' "

Britt said, "Don't say either one. It's none of our business where Mr. Madison's been." I looked at Doris to check her expression after being taken down a notch by one of her brothers.

Pa laughed, "Why, Britt, around here everybody's business is everybody's business. And just for the record, I've been over to Ol' Man Cato's to return his guano distributor and then on into town."

Hoot said, "I didn't mean it as meddlesome, Mr. Madison, when I asked where you been at, I mean, where you was."

Pa laughed again. "I'm pleased you're interested. You might also like to see what Mr. Cato gave me." He turned around and looked back of him, and all of us went onto the road and peeked over the sides of the wagon. There were three big watermelons there, with straw packed under and around them so they wouldn't split open during the bumpy ride. Andrew Jackson was lying there beside them. He didn't bother to open his eyes when we stood over him, but he did thump his tail a time or two against the floor boards.

"They're pretty melons," said Britt.

"Take yourselves one," said Pa. "I had planned to leave one of them here."

"Thank you, sir," said Monroe. "But we've got one

41

a-cooling now." He pointed toward the barrel by the well. "And we'll have more ripe ones in a day or two."

"Then you're ahead of us," said Pa. "We haven't had any yet."

Doris suddenly took an active part in the conversation. "Well, I'll declare," she said. "D. J. was discussing watermelons with us just a little while ago." Everybody sort of giggled except me. I knew she was certain to get even now. She'd tell Pa what I'd said, and I'd regret that I'd ever made up such a story. He's got a special belt he uses on me for lying.

Doris continued, "And we agreed with him that there's nothing better. Won't you all stay and help us eat ours?"

"Thank you, young lady," said Pa, "but we'd best be leaving. It's getting on toward night."

Nutty and I hopped onto the wagon and as Pa drove off, I was careful not to look at Doris. I didn't want her giving me any high-minded glances. Of course, that was silly of me. Down deep I knew that she was a good friend. Maybe I was mainly disgusted with myself for telling a lie that gave her a chance to be decent to me.

I should have said something friendly to all of them as we drove off. Actually, what I said sounded agreeable enough—since they didn't know why I was bringing up the subject. My parting words were: "How are your set hooks? Have you looked at them lately?"

4

THE TRIP

Next morning at sunrise I put on my overalls and went
out to the crib and began loading bags of corn onto
the wagon. In a few minutes, here came Clara May,
swinging a pail in each hand. She was on her way to do
the milking.

At the well, she stopped and drew a bucket of fresh
water. She poured two dipperfuls into the washpan
we kept on a shelf there and rinsed her face and hands.
After she had dried them on the towel that hung from

one of the well's shelter posts, she took up the pails and started away, calling to me, "Good day for us to go to the mill, don't you think?"

I mumbled, "Good day for me and Pa to go."

"Let's don't forget our bathing suits," she answered, and went on into the barn. I heard her carrying on her usual early-morning conversation with the cows. "Get up, Zinnia," she said. "You, too, June-bug. It's not so bad once you get up and stirring."

When she passed along on the way back to the house, I said, "You ain't going with us today. And even if you were, your bathing suit is plumb ragged."

"I don't go swimming to look pretty," she said. Glancing back over her shoulders, she informed me, "I go for the diversion." That's one of the words she took to using in the eighth grade this past year.

At breakfast, Skinny Little Renfroe was being coaxed, as usual, to eat another biscuit. "Put a little thickened gravy on it," said Mamma.

Pa said, "And eat a piece of fatback." That's what we call homegrown bacon. All except Clara May. She thinks it sounds more polite to call it side meat. Pa continued talking to Skinny Little Renfroe. "You'll need plenty of strength for the trip to the mill."

"Aw, Pa!" I said. "He ain't going with us, is he?"

"Why, D. J.! There's plenty of room for everybody."

"We're going to picnic at the millpond," said Mamma, "while the corn's being ground."

I said disgustedly, "The whole family!" That let me in for one of Pa's lectures on me being so selfish and how everybody but me joined in the spirit of things. He said he wished I'd decide to stop being my own worst enemy and enjoy being a part of the family instead. At the end, Skinny Little Renfroe announced: "This is to be a happy day. We'll have us some recreation." He was all the time using the big words that Clara May had toted home from the eighth grade.

After breakfast, I went out to catch the mules. Effie was near the barn and I put a bridle on her and tied her to the pasture gate. Naturally, dopey Twilight was way off in another direction and went on eating grass when I called. You'd have thought she was deaf; she didn't even look up. Then when I got almost to her, she walked away. But she walked into a corner of the pasture, which was poor judgment on her part. It made catching her easy.

Pa was dragging the harness out of the wagon shed when I got back with the mules. Skinny Little Renfroe came out and climbed onto the wagon before it was even hitched up. Next came Andrew Jackson. Neither one of them wanted to risk getting left.

Finally, we got started. Mamma and Pa sat up toward the front on a board that served as the driver's seat. Clara May and I sat at the end of the wagon, dangling our feet over the edge. Skinny Little Renfroe wanted to sit back there with us, but Mamma wouldn't let him. Just before we left home, she had changed the bandage on his foot, which she said looked bad. She didn't want him to get dust in it. Also, she knew about our habit of daring each other to spring off the wagon from time to time when we were sitting there. It wasn't too much fun, nor any trouble, to hop off and back on again if the mules were going slow. But at a good speed, it could be interesting. Pa said it was dangerous, too, and Mamma didn't want to chance Skinny Little Renfroe hurting his foot worse by anything I might dare him to do. So he sat by himself over the rear axle and didn't like it a bit. He looked as droopy as the bag of corn he sat on.

Halfway up the first hill there was a loud scraping noise, sounding as if something had gone wrong with the wheels. Pa stopped the mules and told me to get down and see if I found anything wrong.

After checking carefully, I said, "Something must have got caught in one of the axles, but I guess it dropped out of its own accord." I climbed back up and we started off again.

The sound came again before we reached the top of the hill and we stopped once more to try and find what caused it. Pa climbed down, too, and I stood on one side of the wagon and he stood on the other. He told Ma, "Pull 'er up a bit while we watch for the trouble."

Mamma took up the reins and made a clicking sound to get Effie and Twilight started. Pa and I

46

watched the wheels but couldn't see anything out of the ordinary. He signaled for the mules to be halted, then scratched his head. "I can't figure out what was the trouble," he said.

Skinny Little Renfroe shifted himself over to sit on a different bag of corn and asked, "Did the scraping noise sound like this?" At that, he twisted his mouth to one side and made the screechingest-scrapingest noise I ever did hear.

Pa's face turned white, the way it does when he's exasperated, and his arms flopped to his side. I thought for a minute he was going to collapse in the middle of the road. When the color came back to his face, he said sternly, "Renfroe Madison, I'm a-good mind to make you get out and go home."

Skinny Little Renfroe shivered and looked even smaller than he actually is. "I didn't know it would fool you," he insisted. Of course, I didn't believe him for a minute. He pulled the trick a second time because it had fooled all of us on the first try.

Pa climbed back up onto the seat. "Henceforth," he said, "limit your imitations to the entertaining variety."

"Yes, sir, I will," promised Skinny Little Renfroe, and he cleared his throat and announced loudly: "An imitation. By Renfroe Madison."

I yelled out, "We can get by without it," but he looked down from his perch and told me, "Pa said he wanted to hear one of my imitations."

47

Pa looked around. "No, now Renfroe, I didn't say that." He looked toward the back of the wagon to include me, too, and continued. "We must all learn to represent things straight." His face took on a more agreeable expression and he added, "But now that you've mentioned it, I would sort of like to hear one of your numbers."

Skinny Little Renfroe's face lit up as if he'd been elected President of the United States or something, and he asked, "Which one did you have in mind?"

Pa laughed. "Suit yourself," he said, and we listened for a long time afterwards to what was supposed to sound like three kittens in a pasteboard box. The explanation was: "They're crying because the mamma cat has run off somewhere and they're worried for fear she has gotten herself killed by a mad dog and won't come back to see about them and they'll perish to death unless somebody comes along and feeds them warm milk from an eyedropper."

He was still miaowing when we came in sight of Nutty's house. Nutty was standing by the side of the road, leaning against a post that supported their mailbox. He knew we were going to the mill today, and I had told him to make sure that he happened to be in his front yard. Pa most likely would invite him to come along.

But instead of looking casual, as if he just happened to be on that side of the house, there he stood, propped against a post by the side of the road. His hair was brushed down and he wore clean overalls. Pa stopped the wagon and greeted him. "Would you care to go to the mill with us?" he asked.

"Why, thank you, sir," said Nutty, and he opened the front of the mailbox, pulled out a brown-paper bundle, and headed toward the back of the wagon. Noticing that Pa was looking at the package, he explained, "It's my lunch. I had a feeling somebody might come along and invite me somewhere."

Pa and Mamma laughed and Clara May said, "Run get your bathing suit. We're going swimming in the millpond."

Nutty pulled at the waist of his overalls. "I got it on under here," he said, and hopped aboard.

Pa laughed again. "You were really set for eventualities, weren't you?"

Nutty only grinned, but Skinny Little Renfroe wanted to know what eventualities meant. It was explained to him as we rode along. He listened so carefully that I knew we could expect to hear him using it every time he opened his mouth from now on.

Nutty and I bounced on and off the wagon a couple of times soon after we got underway, but the mules weren't going fast enough for it to be any fun. We tried again when we came to a downhill slope and the wagon gathered speed. The first time we jogged off, we got back on again easy enough. But the second time, I misgauged the speed of the wagon and lost my footing. Nutty dropped back to see if I was hurt, and when he saw that I wasn't, we both started running. We kept losing ground and finally called out to Pa to wait for us. Clara May and Skinny Little Renfroe, of course, had been watching us, but they hadn't told what was going on at the back of the wagon. It was our system.

Pa looked around when we yelled, but seeing that we were able to run he did not slow down the mules.

5

"THERE AIN'T NOTHING LIKE A GOOD FIGHT"

We weren't the only folks who had decided it would be a good day to come to the mill. Four wagons were ahead of us, but they had already been unloaded and were out by the hitching rails. The miller showed us where to pile our corn and said it would be midafternoon, or thereabouts, before he could grind it.

We started then on the unloading. Pa said he was tempted to make me and Nutty do it by ourselves as punishment for springing off the wagon. "I don't know," he added. "Maybe I've already impressed on you the foolishness of your act." He had let us run half a mile before slowing the wagon down enough for us to catch it; that's how he'd impressed us. Anyway, he helped unload the corn, too. We toted it from the wagon to the spot the miller had pointed out.

Just as I put down the last bag, a booming voice warned, "Hey, Buster, watch where you're putting that sack!" I looked up and saw a big, red-faced man.

Pa appeared in a flash. "What's the matter?" he asked.

The man said, "That boy was putting your corn too near mine." Evidently, his supply was against the wall ahead of ours.

Pa said, "Excuse him, Ratty. He didn't realize it was too close."

So this was Ratty Logan. At least, I felt sure that's who it was—surely there wasn't anybody else named Ratty in the whole world—and I looked up to see him better. All my life I'd heard of Ratty Logan, but I'd never seen him before. It would have suited me better now if he'd been at more of a distance. He was so close he could have reached out and hit me, and from all I'd heard about him, he wouldn't hesitate to do something like that.

He said, "Last time I brought corn to be ground, somebody stole two bags of it."

"Well," said Pa, "my son wasn't trying to take anything from you."

Ratty mumbled, "I don't trust nobody," and Pa and I left to go see about the wagon. I saw that Skinny Little Renfroe had been standing in the doorway watching, and as soon as we were out of earshot of the mill, he asked Pa, "Was that really Ratty?"

"Yes, siree, that was really Ratty," answered Pa. "And he's running true to form."

We tied up the wagon over at the hitching rails and all of us except Andrew Jackson got out. He never got out until we were home again, if he could help it. The rest of us walked out to the lake above the dam. A man there was catching shiners, one after another, as fast as he could bait his hook. Pa said, "If I'd known fish were biting, I'd have brought along my tackle."

Mamma reported, "The almanac says the moon's not right," and the man said he reckoned shiners didn't read the almanac. He offered to lend Pa a spare pole and line.

"Thank you, no," said Pa. "I'd better walk down below the dam with the young 'uns and see that none of them drown in the millpond."

That sent all of us chasing back to the wagon to get our bathing suits. Mamma called to Skinny Little Renfroe to wait a minute. But he was hobbling as fast as the rest of us could run, and was up on the wagon quick as a wink, emptying out the bag of bathing suits.

"Here's yours," he called to Clara May, throwing her moth-eaten one to her. "And here's yours, D. J.," he added, pitching me my new trunks. They were one of the things I'd bought for myself with the money I'd earned chopping cotton. Then he tossed out a towel or two.

"What?" he said, looking distressed. "Mine's not in here." After a few seconds, he put the bag down and appeared happier. "I'll just swim in my underwear," he said, which was what he and I had both done once when we forgot our suits.

Mamma said, "No, I think you'd better not go in. I didn't bring your suit because we can't risk a foot infection."

"Oh, I won't catch any infection," he insisted, and Mamma tried to convince him that she was thinking about what was best for him. She also reminded him that she had told him this before we left home, but he had pretended not to be listening. He has a way of thinking that if he doesn't admit to hearing anything he doesn't want to hear that everything will be all right. While they talked, Clara May went into a clump of scrub pines and put on her bathing suit. I put on mine on the other side of the wagon and Nutty stripped down to his and we headed for the millpond.

The only other place we've ever been swimming is the river, and we're partial to the millpond. It's 'most

54

always clear and there's not much trash in it. Also, it gets deep gradually and the bottom is sandy instead of muddy and doesn't have any potholes in it.

While we were swimming, Skinny Little Renfroe was fit to be tied. "I'll just go wading," he said, and had one foot almost in the water before Mamma could stop him. He pouted for a while, then began to feel better when we let him judge the races between Nutty and me and Clara May. We tried to see which one of us could swim across from the opposite bank fastest. I won the first two races, and Nutty won the last one. Clara May didn't win any and said it was on account of her bathing suit straps kept slipping down over her arms and hindering her.

After the swim, we ate lunch. We wanted to go swimming again afterwards but Mamma and Pa said, "No." It might give us cramps or something. We said we hadn't eaten all that much, but it didn't sway them. We gave up when Nutty found an old beanbag in a wagon rut and suggested that we play keep-away.

Skinny Little Renfroe said, "That's a good idea," and went hobbling out across a cleared-off space. "Here, Nutty, throw it to me," he yelled. "Let's you and me keep it away from D. J. and Clara."

Nutty threw the bag to him, and Clara May went chasing after it like a wild woman. "Come on, D. J.," she called. "Do your part!"

But I didn't move, and they all stopped to see what was the matter. "Ain't you gonna play with us?" asked Skinny Little Renfroe.

"Nutty and I are going exploring," I said. "We don't care for keep-away."

"Don't we?" asked Nutty, as if he hadn't been the one to suggest it in the first place.

I insisted that he and I would have a better time by ourselves. I thought Pa was going to say that as usual everybody but me had a proper outlook and suggest that I try being a part of the family instead of always against it. But he said since this was somewhat of a holiday for all of us, he supposed I ought to be allowed to do as I pleased. So he let Nutty and me go off to the woods at the head of the lake to see what was there, while Clara May and Skinny Little Renfroe walked out toward the main road. They wanted to see who would be aboard the wagons that were headed toward the mill.

Nutty and I walked along the edge of the lake, hoping we'd see a muskrat or a beaver. But all we saw were tadpoles and little fish in the shallow water. We found an old tin can and tried to catch some of the fish. Nutty thought they might be a special kind that grew here and that we should take a few home and put them in the river. That would give us a start of something new to mix with the mudcats and suckers that were the main kind there. But the longer we tried to catch the fish, the trickier they became about getting away. Several times we had two or three of them almost hemmed in, then they'd scoot around the can and be gone. Finally, we gave up and decided to roam around the woods for a while.

We hadn't come onto anything interesting by the time the gong sounded at the mill. Pa had said that would be the way he'd signal to us when it was time to come back.

As we went along, I tried to make up something we could tell the others about what we had seen while exploring. Nutty didn't see any harm in telling the truth, and I had to waste valuable time explaining to him that you just don't do that—not when you've got a nosy sister and brother who'd say you would have had more fun throwing a beanbag. "I'll make up a whopper or two," I said, just as we got back to the mill. "And you stick by me, understand?"

Clara May greeted us. "You really missed something!" she said, and Skinny Little Renfroe added, "We saw a sight to see!" They were feeding Twilight and Effie an armful of grass.

I would have thought they were making up a tale so we'd be sorry we hadn't joined in their games, but they both looked too excited to be pretending. Also, Jeff Carlton, a boy in my grade at school, was balancing

57

himself on the wheel of the wagon next to ours. He called out. "We saw a fight better than anything you and I ever got into on the schoolyard."

"Mr. Ratty Logan got his head stuck in that pile of corncobs over yonder," said Skinny Little Renfroe. He pointed in the direction of the cobs from the mill that were deposited in a stack half as tall as a house.

Nutty asked, "How could he get his head stuck in a pile of corncobs?"

"On account of Mr. Grady Clay knocked him down and stuck his head in 'em."

Jeff came over and joined in describing what had happened. "They got in a squabble inside the mill," he said, "and the miller told them that if they wanted to fight to go outside."

"And that's what they did," said Clara May, "and we all watched."

Skinny Little Renfroe added, "It sure was a good one."

"There ain't nothing like a good fight," said Jeff. "And that was the best one I ever saw." Then he told how my pa and his pa had stopped it after a while, but not until Mr. Clay and Ratty had been given time to have themselves a pretty nice brawl. Jeff said, "Mr. Clay's probably the only man around here who can whip Ratty singlehanded."

Pa came out of the mill then and Mamma came over from where she had been chatting with some women across the yard, and we drove around to the loading platform. Jeff helped us and it took only a few minutes to load the wagon. It's always surprising how the corn, in being ground, dwindles down to such a small amount of meal.

We piled in and got started for home. Jeff followed us to the road, telling more details of the fight that he thought Nutty and I should hear. After he turned back, Clara May continued to talk about it. Whenever she came to a part that needed sound effects, she would call on Skinny Little Renfroe. And he would render an imitation entitled: Ratty Logan sputtering while Mr. Grady Clay held his head in the corncobs.

I thought again of maybe telling a lie or two about the adventures Nutty and I had not had on our jaunt. But I had sense enough to know that anything I could make up would not compare with what they had seen. And so did they.

I expected them to come straight out and ask: "Now don't you wish you had played keep-away with us?" But instead, Skinny Little Renfroe looked down from his seat, a turned-up bucket wedged between the bags of meal, and said, "Too bad you missed out on the eventualities."

6

THE SNAKE

The next morning at the table Skinny Little Renfroe said he couldn't eat all of his egg because his foot hurt. "I expect you played on it too hard yesterday," said Mamma. "But it won't keep you from eating. You need the nourishment."

He ate another bite and then said he believed he would go outdoors, but Mamma told him to wait. She wanted to have a look at his ankle.

As soon as breakfast was over, she sat him down on the back porch and took off the bandage. She examined the wound carefully. "I don't like the looks of these streaks shooting out from it," she said, and sent me to fetch a washpan and Clara May to get a kettle of hot water and the box of salt. She thought Skinny Little Renfroe should soak his foot for a while, but he was not easy to convince. He would stick one toe in the water and complain that it was too hot. Next he would complain that it was too cold, and once he said it was too salty. Mamma coaxed him until he eventually put his whole foot in the pan.

Clara May and I got set to go to the vegetable garden. I began rounding up baskets and buckets while she hunted for her straw hat. Mamma said, "Wear my sun bonnet," but Clara May kept looking till she found her own hat.

"I'm going with you," said Skinny Little Renfroe. "I can pick the butter beans."

"Good," said Clara May. "And I'll pick the tomatoes, and D. J. will gather the corn and cut the okra."

"Oh, no, I won't," I said. "*You* cut the okra this time." The scratchy okra pods and leaves bring on itching. That's why it's not one of our favorite vegetables to gather. We feel the same way about squash and cucumbers, but we weren't to gather them this morning—just the things that could go into soup mixture.

Mamma said, "Renfroe, you'd better not go. There's still dew on the ground and we must keep your bandage dry."

Naturally, he argued for a while, but finally gave up. Looking as if the end of the world were coming, he asked, "If I got dew in my sore foot, would I die?"

"Why, no, child," said Mamma. "But it's not wise to take chances."

He appeared depressed, but later in the morning when we returned from the garden, he was cheerful again. I put a bucket of tomatoes onto the end of the porch and he imitated Ratty Logan: "Hey, Buster, watch where you're putting that bucket!" He and Clara May laughed like crazy folks.

Just to get even, I looked him straight in the eyes and said, "Mamma can't tell you whether you're gonna die or not. Nobody ever knows."

The troubled expression returned to his face, and I was sorry at once that I had said anything worrisome. But Clara May made him feel better. "If you're thinking about going to Glory right away," she said, "all I've got to say is that it's poor timing on your part. You know good and well that *you-know-what* will arrive most any day now."

That brought on a big grin from him.

Pa was late coming home for lunch and after the cooking was finished, Mamma and Clara May came into the yard. We all sat under the pecan tree and waited. It was cooler there than inside the house.

Skinny Little Renfroe felt called upon to show off. "I'll favor us with my newest imitation," he said.

"Don't bother," I said, but Mamma encouraged him to go ahead and favor us.

"Well," he said, "it's going to be a billy goat and a nanny goat and a baby goat and one or two more goats bleating at the feed-room door on account of it's past suppertime and the boy who's supposed to feed them didn't get there yet because he went to the fair and ran out of money and couldn't pay his way back by bus and is having to walk home." It would seem that he would have been out of breath by then, but he didn't even slow down. "See if you can guess which one's the baby," he said, and set in bleating—and was still at it when Pa come along.

"I thought a herd of goats had overrun us," said Pa, and everybody laughed as we went inside to eat.

During the meal, Pa told us about a snake he had killed that morning. He reported, "It was at the edge of the far field, in among those mulberry saplings." He went on to tell how he had been working nearby, trying to dig out a clump of persimmon sprouts, when he spied the snake. "At first I thought it was a root of one of the mulberries, the way they sometimes spread out along the top of the ground. But when it began to wriggle I knew it wasn't any root! Then it slithered

63

into a better light and I could see the markings down its back. I knew it was the biggest highland moccasin I ever saw." He told how he had eased away at that point to look for a long stick.

"Why didn't you kill it with the mattock?" asked Clara May.

"The handle's too short. The snake would have been gone before I could get close enough to kill it with the mattock. So I found a big stick and WHAM, I hit it a good 'un."

Mamma said, "Well, I hope you gave it more than one lick."

"Don't worry," said Pa. "That's one snake that ain't gonna get up and move about after I killed it."

We all laughed, thinking back about the time Pa came in the house saying he had killed a coachwhip at our back steps. But when we all ran to the door to look out, the snake he had "killed" had revived itself and was scurrying under the smokehouse.

Pa insisted the one today was good and dead. "But it sure does alarm me," he said, "to see a moccasin of that size around here." Sounding sterner than usual, he cautioned all of us to keep our eyes open and to be extremely careful about where we stepped. Naturally, none of us wear shoes in the summertime. In fact, we don't have any. We always get a pair in the fall, and they are generally worn out or outgrown, or both, by warm weather—which is all right, because they're not needed again until winter. But Clara May's planning to buy hers this year at the end of summer. She says the rest of the girls in the ninth grade will start right out wearing shoes on the first day of school, and she will too. Clara May's prissy.

In the afternoon, Nutty and I fooled around down by the spring for a while, then I talked him into us taking a hike over to the far field. We could have a look at the moccasin Pa had killed.

Out at the road, we met Clara May on the way home from the mailbox. Nutty asked, "Where's Renfroe?"

"He was with me," she answered, "but he saw a chipmunk on the way home and went running into the woods to try and catch it. If you all see him, remind him to keep the bandage tied around his foot." She added, as she started away, "I have to go help Mamma can soup mixture."

Mamma is a big believer in soup mixture. She's convinced that it's what kept us from starving two years ago. That was the time Pa had to borrow money to buy seed and fertilizer to plant his crops. During the summer a woman from the County Agent's office came out to show Mamma how to can soup mixture and things like that. It was a way of storing up vegetables while they were plentiful against a time when there wouldn't be a sprig of anything growing. Skinny

Little Renfroe was three and a half then and used to speak of the "soup mystery." He doesn't make mistakes like that any more. In fact, sometimes it seems that he's a whole lot older than he is. I'm not sure he's not a freak.

"Let's take the short cut," suggested Nutty, and we left the road and cut across the bottom lands. Actually, it's not a short cut, but it's a good way to get to the far field, all the same. When we came to the creek we swung out over it on muscadine vines that drooped down from a water oak. The idea was to catch hold of one of the vines and shove off with enough force to land on the opposite bank. But it was more fun to hang on for the return trip, too, so we played for a while before we officially crossed to the other side and went on to the field.

At the mulberry saplings, I concerned myself about where I put down my bare feet. Not that I'm squeamish, but I *had* promised Pa to be careful. The pokeweeds and honeysuckle vines were so thick that it was hard to see the ground. It gave me an eerie feeling. The thought of a dead snake didn't bother me as much as the possibility that a live one might be hunting for it. I've heard strange tales about snakes and how their mates sometimes hang around the one that dies.

"Here it is," called Nutty, excitedly, from over on the other side of the biggest sapling. I forgot about being careful where I stepped and rushed over to have a look. "No, it's not, either," he said, "it's one of the roots of this ol' mulberry." We were both disgusted that he had been mistaken.

We went on searching for a long time and never did find a thing. "Ain't that just like Pa!" I said, knowing, of course, that it was not at all like Pa. The snake in our yard had been a coachwhip and of not much consequence one way or another, but a highland moccasin was as poisonous as they come. Pa would have made certain he had killed it. On the other hand, it wasn't anywhere to be seen, and if it had come alive and was anywhere in this underbrush, I was ready to get out to where we could see the ground better. Nutty favored it, too, and we moseyed back toward home.

It was one of those quiet days when everything seems to be lying low on account of it's so hot. I don't think we even saw a bird in the woods, and I know we didn't scare up a rabbit. The only thing to do was to make our way to the spring. We could have a drink of water and sit around where it was cooler till time to do the late afternoon chores.

At the spring, I took down the gourd dipper from the big rock and was kneeling at the water's edge when I saw something under the big oak that made me jump. Nutty saw it at the same time and whispered, "That's not any tree root!"

"No, it's not," I said, and we both eased back a distance so we wouldn't scare the snake we had seen.

We hurried over to a sycamore tree that the lightning had struck last year and found a big limb that had fallen from it. "We'll sneak back," I said. "Then when we're near enough, I'll flail it with this limb and you can stone it." Nutty was agreeable to the plan and in no time had himself a double handful of rocks and a pocketful besides.

We started back, and in spite of the heat I felt little chills along my neck. We eased forward slowly, and when at last we were in range, I held the limb high and BLAM, I struck the moccasin powerfully. Then I hit it another time and then another. All the while, Nutty was peppering it with rocks, and he's got good aim. Neither of us slowed down until we had beaten the snake so much it couldn't possibly still be alive. Then we gave it a few more licks for good measure and stepped back and caught our breath.

Just as I was about to turn the snake over to have a better look, there was a splash in the spring behind us.

"What was that?" I asked.

Nutty thought it might be another snake, and we looked in the water. A green acorn came floating to the top. While we were standing there, another acorn came down with more force than natural. We looked up and saw Skinny Little Renfroe out on the big low limb, grinning down at us. He then dropped a handful of acorns to the ground.

"What are you doing up there?" I asked crossly.

"Just sitting in a tree," was his stupid answer. "What are you all doing down there?"

I wasn't going to even answer him. Any fool would have known that he couldn't have helped seeing everything we had been doing. But dumb Nutty said, "We killed a snake!"

"Did you, sure enough?" said Skinny Little Renfroe, climbing across the limb. "I'm coming down to see it."

We were looking at the snake closer by the time he got down from the tree and he hobbled over to where we stood. The bandage on his foot had almost been torn off by a snag he struck on the tree.

"That's a big 'un, ain't it?" he said, going over to a spot near a log and brushing dead leaves aside. Finding the end of a string there, he picked it up and gave it a pull. At the same time the snake moved forward.

I was grabbing for the limb to hit it again when I saw what was happening. The other end of the string was tied around the snake, just back of its head.

I knew right off what had happened, but Nutty can't figure things out as fast as I can so I had to clear it up for him. "Skinny Little Renfroe beat us over to the far field and found the snake and dragged it over here."

This played right into Skinny Little Renfroe's hands. "Did you all go looking for it too?" he asked, and I wished that I hadn't admitted we had even been interested in it.

He said, "I went on over there after I chased a chipmunk nearly that far." He gave every detail of his trip, telling exactly where he located the snake. "I was dragging it back so Mamma and Clara May could see it," he said, "but along the way I had an idea about tricking whoever came to the spring first. I'm glad it turned out the way it did."

Nutty said, "If that was the snake your pa killed, how come we thought it was alive?"

Skinny Little Renfroe took credit quickly. "On account of I did such a good job scattering leaves around the beat-up places on it."

I was aggravated, but Nutty laughed. He said, "Renfroe, you're better at thinking up meanness than we are. Maybe you ought to join up with us regular."

I groaned, knowing how this was apt to go to his head. He would start thinking more than ever that he was supposed to tag around everywhere with me. I looked over at him, confident he would be grinning himself silly, but he wasn't. A pained expression was on his face and his eyes watered as if tears were forming in them. "What's the matter?" I asked. "We ain't mad with you."

He sniffed but did not begin to cry. "My foot hurts," he said, sounding scared. He touched the calf of his leg. "All of a sudden it hurts clear up to here." He started to take a step and made an awful face.

"I'll help you to the house," I said, "and Mamma can fix it for you."

He looked around and I thought he was going to say he had rather Nutty help him. Instead, he said, "Nutty, what about you dragging the snake so Mamma and Clara May can see it?" Then he held onto me so he wouldn't have to put his weight on the leg that hurt. His left arm was clinging around my neck and he patted my shoulder and said, "But I won't tell them about me tricking you and Nutty. They might tease you."

"Aw, that's all right," I said, which was being a better sport than I sometimes am. But he looked so pitiful when we started out—and seemed so little and frail leaning up against me for support—that I wanted to cheer him up if I could. "They'll think it was a good joke," I added, and he grinned until another pain caught him.

The red streaks on his legs were prominent, looking much worse than they had that morning. Mamma appeared upset when she saw them. "I'll get some warm salt water," she said. "But maybe we'd better have Dr. Coe take a look too."

This worried me because we almost never go to the doctor. "Want me to go hitch up the wagon?" I asked.

Mamma looked again at the leg. "No," she said, "I think we'd better ask the doctor to come out here this time. Catch one of the mules and ride into town to fetch him." I headed across the yard and she called after me, "Tell him to hurry."

7

TWILIGHT,
THE UNPREDICTABLE MULE

Sometimes I get the feeling that animals have a way of knowing more than folks think. Twilight, for instance, is the most contrary mule there ever was. Usually, when I want to catch her, she has other ideas. But when I don't want to catch her, she sometimes follows me around the pasture like a puppy dog.

When Mamma sent me to fetch the doctor, I knew ol' Twilight would act up because I was in such a rush. I grabbed the bridle from the peg in the wagon shed and hurried out to run her down. But there she stood at the pasture gate. And when I started to put the bit in her mouth, she took it as if she was hoping I had come to get her.

That's why I thought she must have known we had us an urgent task. I also figured she knew it was her friend, Skinny Little Renfroe, who was needing help. All the animals around the place liked him, but I'll just bet that if it had been me who was sick, Twilight would be chasing around the pasture till yet.

Anyway, she let me climb on her back and then struck out. She wouldn't even slow down at the corner post where I kept burlap bags for use as a saddle whenever I had to ride any distance. So I rode on without them.

Andrew Jackson had been stretched out beside the road, sleeping in the shade of a black walnut tree, but he got to his feet and barked at us. It's probably the only time he has ever stirred himself in the heat of the afternoon to bark at anything. I figured he sensed something was wrong, also, and was warning Twilight that Skinny Little Renfroe was worse off than we thought and for her to get me into town in a hurry. At least, that's what I thought the message had been, and from the way Twilight was galloping, she must have understood it. She was kicking up a trail of red dust when we were traveling by the Castor place. And 'most all the Castors were in sight. Monroe was chopping kindling and Hoot was stacking it up, while Britt and Chester were hoeing around cantaloupes beside the road. Doris was sweeping their back yard with a brush broom.

Every one of them waved at me and yelled, "Howdy, D. J." I was jogging up and down too fast to think of anything mean to call out to them so I yelled "Howdy" back. What was worse, I took one hand off the reins to wave, and when I did—I fell off. I don't know exactly how I lost my balance, but all of a sudden I was sitting in a clump of Johnson grass by the side of the road instead of atop Twilight.

I wasn't hurt, but the fall must have stunned me because before I got to my feet, all four of the Castor boys had gathered around me.

Naturally, Chester was the one who had to comment on the situation. He said, "It appears you fell off."

"How'd you figure that out?" I asked, getting up to run after Twilight. She was halfway up the next hill and I yelled at her as loud as I could. I don't know if she heard me or just suddenly realized I wasn't still with her, but something caused her to turn around and come back down the road. I ran to meet her, glad to get away from all those Castors. But when she reached me, she kept going. Chester and Britt slowed her down when she got to them, and Monroe walked up to her and took hold of the rope. Of course, I had to go back to where they stood.

74

Doris called out, "That was a real good trick you did a while ago, D. J. Let's see you do it again."

All of them laughed and I swung up on Twilight without saying a word, slapped her flank, and we were off to a swift start—in the wrong direction. Finally, I managed to turn her around and she moved fast enough until we passed that line of Castors again. Then she dragged along at such a pace that Chester had time to tell me about a turtle they caught. "It was the biggest one we've ever laid eyes on."

"And good, too," added Britt. "We had it for supper last night."

"We caught it on a set hook," continued Chester. "Somehow a dead crow got snagged on the hook and it served as bait for the turtle. Did you ever hear of such a thing?"

Twilight spared me the trouble of having to answer. She struck out running when I gouged my heels into her ribs.

In town, I went straight to Dr. Coe's house. I rode into the side yard and was tying Twilight to a china-berry tree when a woman warned me from a window that I was standing in her flowers. That sent me to the back yard, where another woman was hanging a mop onto a rack nailed to the buggy shelter. Dr. Coe had himself a car, but he still kept a horse and buggy for seasons of the year when the roads are too muddy for anything else.

75

"Is Dr. Coe at home?" I asked.

"I'm the housekeeping staff, child," she said pleasantly. "You'd better ask at the front door about doctoring business," so I went around to the front and rang the bell.

The woman who had said I was standing in her flowers came to the door, appearing more agreeable than I thought she would. "The doctor is out on a call," she said. "You may wait for him, if you'd like, or I'll give him your message."

"Maybe I'd better wait," I said, and went out to the corner of the yard and sat on a bench under a cottonwood tree.

A scrawny looking girl with pigtails played with a ball in the next yard. She was my age, or maybe a year or two younger, and kept bouncing the ball nearer and nearer to where I sat. She made out like she didn't see me, and whenever I'd look at her, she would gaze off somewhere else. But she came closer and closer until she was under the cottonwood, standing directly in front of me. Then she pretended to be surprised. "Hey there!" she said. "I didn't see you over here."

"Howdy," I said, sounding as growly as I could. It ought to have let her know I'd just as soon be left alone, but she hugged the ball to herself and stared at me. Eventually she said, "My name's Clydie Sue."

I said, without looking up, "Who said it weren't?"

and she went back to bouncing the ball in her own yard.

In a few minutes Dr. Coe came motoring into the driveway in his brand new Model A Ford. It was one of the finest looking cars I've ever seen, not that I've seen many cars. "Yes, sir, young man," the doctor said, "what can I do for you?"

While I told him what was wrong, he opened his satchel and seemed to be paying more attention to it than to what I was saying. But I realized he was listening when I got to the part about the streaks running up Skinny Little Renfroe's leg. A frown came over his face.

"I'll get right out there," he said. "Do you want to ride with me, or is that your mule tied up in the back yard?"

"Yes, sir," I said. "That's her."

Dr. Coe smiled. "Well, I reckon there's not room in the car for both of you," he said, and got into his Model A. In almost no time he had it cranked up and backed around and headed toward the road.

Twilight evidently knew our job was done, because she went back to being her contrary self. She snorted and pulled at the rope while I was untying her, as if she couldn't wait to get going. Then when I climbed on her back, she poked along the driveway so slowly I thought she would keel over dead. The girl with the pigtails was at the edge of the next yard, looking up at me.

"So long, Clydie Sue," I said, sort of half-friendly.

She answered, "Mamma don't allow me to associate with *country* children."

I thought to myself: Ain't that the way of it? She wanted to be friendly earlier and I acted smart-alecky. Now it was the other way around. I would have kept going and not said anything, but Twilight balked. Maybe even she resented it when anybody said *country* as if it were a bad word. Before I could say anything, Clydie Sue continued. "I'll bet you've got barnyard dirt sticking between your toes," she said, looking at my bare feet. It was none of her business that they could have used a good scrubbing.

"This town ain't a whole lot different from the country," I said, regretting at once that I was bothering to put up a defense. I looked toward the barn and paddock at the end of her yard. "Ain't that a horse grazing back yonder?"

"There's a difference 'twixt a horse and a mule," she said, snippy-like. "And besides, Pa's gonna buy an automobile any day now."

I said flatly, "Mine's gonna buy *two*," which was a lie, of course. Then I asked, "How about that cow back there? I suppose you keep her just to look pretty."

Clydie Sue lifted her shoulders and said, "We *hire* the milking done."

That was too much for Twilight. She started off at a gallop, without giving me time to say another word. I started to turn around and yell something back, but I didn't want to risk getting thrown off again. So I held my head high and rode away as if this galloping were my idea instead of Twilight's.

It was late afternoon when I passed back along the Castor place. Hoot was out shelling corn for the chickens, while his baby sisters stayed busy scaring them away. Doris was taking down washing from the clothes line and Chester was drawing water at the well. Britt and Monroe must have been inside the barn, milking.

Mrs. Castor looked out from the kitchen door and motioned for me to wait a minute. "I just wanted to find out if everybody's all right at your house," she said, after I'd ridden up to meet her. "Dr. Coe drove past here not long ago and I was afraid somebody might be sick in your family or at the Gilfords." The Gilfords are Nutty and his grandpa and grandma.

"The trouble's at our house," I said, and went on to tell her about it. Folks around here do most of their own doctoring, and that's why they know something serious has happened when they see a real doctor coming to call.

I started to leave then and Mrs. Castor called after me, "Tell your ma to let me know if I can be of any help."

"Thank you, ma'am," I answered, and went along home.

At the watering trough, Twilight drank her fill. Then I put her in the barn and threw down an armful of hay from the loft and brought her a few nubbins from the crib. I could still hear her chomping on the corn when I got to the porch.

Inside, Clara May was at the kitchen stove cooking supper. I walked to the bedroom where Mamma was talking to Dr. Coe. Skinny Little Renfroe was piled up in the bed, a sheet pulled around him. His head was on a feather pillow and he looked as if he had been bleached as white as the bed covers.

Mamma said to me, "I hope you didn't turn Twilight back in the pasture." I told her I hadn't, and she explained, "Dr. Coe has prescribed some medicine that he doesn't have in his pill case. But he'll get it at the drugstore in town and you're to bring it home."

The doctor fastened a strap around his satchel and said, "If you've got the strength to walk back out here, you could ride into town with me."

I was quick to answer, "Oh, I've got the strength."

Mamma said she reckoned that it would be as good and as speedy a system as muleback both ways. "Your Pa will see to your night chores when he comes in from the fields, but don't tarry along the way, even so."

I said to the doctor, "I never have rid in an automobile."

Clara May corrected me from the kitchen. *"Ridden,"* she called.

At the mention of an automobile, Skinny Little Renfroe's eyes opened wide and he pushed himself up in the bed. "Maybe I could come too," he said. "I'm feeling a whole lot better."

8

THE YOU-KNOW-WHAT

Dr. Coe started back to town, me sitting on the seat beside him as if I had been riding in automobiles all my life. He took the road that went past the Gilfords' place and I concentrated on Nutty being out near the road. I wanted him to see me motoring by. Sure enough, he was out there, but instead of waving, as I'd planned, I felt urged to see if he couldn't share in all this excitement.

The motor was making a lot of noise and it was not

easy to be heard above it while jostling along, but I said loudly, pointing to Nutty at the same time, "I don't suppose you've got room to let him go too."

It was a foolish thing to say, since the whole back seat was empty. I ought to have said something like, "Would it inconvenience you to let that boy over there take a ride with us?" But I don't always think up exactly what's a good way to put something until after I've said it.

Dr. Coe pressed down on his brakes, which caught so sharply I nearly hit the windshield. He said, "I suppose we can squeeze him in," and motioned for Nutty to come along.

"How you get in this thing?" asked Nutty, pulling at a lever on the outside.

"Push it the other way," called Dr. Coe, and Nutty finally got the handle down and hopped onto the back seat. He slammed the door so hard behind him that the car rocked. I looked to see if Dr. Coe was frowning, but he didn't seem upset as we started off.

Nutty bounced up and down a time or two. "This sets good," he said, and bounced once more. "The springs don't squeak like our buggy seat," he said, and then leaned up over us and peered at the steering wheel and the rest of the driving apparatus. "This is a fine car," he said, as if all cars weren't fine.

"Thank you," said Dr. Coe.

"How much did it cost?" asked Nutty, and I no-

83

ticed that the doctor's smile disappeared. I decided I'd better answer the question.

"You're not supposed to ask folks how much things cost," I said, sounding for all the world like Clara May correcting me. I hated to do it to Nutty, but I figured it was better than letting him aggravate the doctor.

"Ain't you?" he said.

The doctor laughed and we all sat back and relaxed. Only Nutty relaxed too much. I peeked around and saw what he was doing. He didn't hold onto the seat the way I did, or try to steady himself whenever the car struck bumpy places in the road, which was often. Instead of bracing himself, he held his hands out loose to the side, as if he wanted to be bounced off the seat. I wouldn't put it past him to have been lifting his feet off the floor, too.

After each bounce, he'd land back on the seat with a thud that reminded me of the time I had jogged up and down on a bed at home until the slats fell out. I'd been little then, but I'd gotten a whipping, for sure. I didn't know what Nutty would get if he didn't try bracing himself. That's what I was thinking about when we struck a washboardy place in the road and suddenly one bump was the worst yet and I heard a loud CLUNK. The timing wasn't right for Nutty to be landing and I knew right off what had happened. He had hit his head on the overhead of the car. He was rubbing his forehead and shaking his head at the same time. Dr. Coe stopped the car and turned around. "Lean up here and let me have a look," he said.

Nutty sat forward. "The skin's not broken," said the doctor. "If there's a knot by the time we get to town, I'll find something to put on it." He didn't add, "From now on, hold tight!" but I noticed that Nutty sat firm during the rest of the trip.

At the drugstore, we all went inside and the doctor ordered the medicine I was to take home. While the druggist was rolling the pills, Dr. Coe took a bottle of something out of his satchel and rubbed the bruised spot on Nutty's head.

By then, the druggist had our medicine ready. The doctor told him to "put it on the books" and that he or Pa would settle for it later. "But I'll pay cash for a dime's worth of stick candy," he added, "if you'll put it in two sacks and throw in a few silver bells extra."

When the candy was counted out, Dr. Coe handed both sacks of it to me. "One is for the two of you to eat on the way home," he said, "and the other one is for your little brother. Maybe it'll help make up for the bad taste of the pills."

We thanked him kindly for the candy and for the ride into town, and Nutty asked if there were any charges for doctoring his head. I don't know, offhand, what he would have done if the answer had been "Yes." He probably would have asked for it to be put on the books. But the doctor said, "No charge for

85

knots on the head that come from riding in my car."
Then he told us to get along home and to tell Mamma
he would come out the next day to check on his pa-
tient.

The walk home was something of a let-down from
the classy way we had ridden into town, but the candy
helped our spirits. It ran out before the journey was
over and the thought occurred to me to dip into the
sack that was not ours—that maybe Skinny Little
Renfroe ought not to eat any candy. But since the
doctor had sent it, that line of figuring didn't hold up
very well, and I managed to get home without borrow-
ing so much as one silver bell.

The rest of the family had finished supper when I
got there, and mine was in the warming closet of the
stove. While I ate it, Mamma and Pa and Clara May
asked if I'd seen anybody or heard any news worth re-
peating on my two trips to town that day. Skinny Little
Renfroe was napping, but at bedtime Mamma woke
him up to take one of his pills. When he saw me crawling into the other bed in our room, he revived enough
to wash down the pill with a swallow of water and to
ask about the ride to town. He wanted to know if the
doctor had had any trouble holding the car in the road,
and had anybody fallen out.

The next day he had to stay in bed the whole time.
The medicine had made him drowsy and he didn't put
up much argument about not being allowed up. Dr.

Coe came back in the afternoon and didn't have much to say, but he looked mighty solemn while he was doing his examining. And when he was out of the room, I saw him shaking his head.

But the next day Skinny Little Renfroe was wide-awake and asked at least once every fifteen minutes if it was time to go for the mail—and could he get out of bed and go with Clara May to fetch it. He insisted that he would walk mostly on his good foot, barely touching the tip of the other one to the ground.

Mamma said, "Absolutely not!" and wouldn't change her mind, no matter how much he begged. Clara May helped his feelings, though, when she was leaving. "If *you-know-what* gets here," she said, "I won't open it till I get home. And I'll hurry back."

She set out for the mailbox then and it was sort of unfortunate that their package did arrive that day. As many times as Skinny Little Renfroe had trailed along after her in the hopes that they would have this big whatever-it-was waiting for them, it was too bad he missed out on going for it. But Clara May, always as good as her word, came flying back with it still unopened.

I was sitting on the back steps, whittling a willow whistle I was making for Skinny Little Renfroe, when she came in. I barely looked up, but I could tell how excited she was. She said, "You can come in and see it as soon as we get it unpacked," sounding as if she thought that was the main thing that was on my mind. Then I heard her closing the door to the room where Skinny Little Renfroe was resting.

I gave them about a minute and then went inside and busted into the room. I expected them both to yell that it wasn't time yet, but they were so busy admiring their purchase that they forgot to be cross that they hadn't sent for me.

"Come look!" said Clara May, and Skinny Little Renfroe added, "Ain't it pretty?"

"A radio!" I said. "You didn't have enough money to buy a radio."

Skinny Little Renfroe said happily, "It's a cheap one."

"Inexpensive," corrected Clara May, not ever being so carried away with anything that she forgot to correct our grammar at the same time.

"That's what I mean," said Skinny Little Renfroe. "It's an inexpensive one. But ain't it pretty? See if you can turn it on, Clara May."

She looked at the front of it and I said, "Turn that knob on the right till it clicks." Clara May turned it on and then we waited.

After several minutes went by, she said, "It ought to be warmed up by now."

"Turn the other knob till that needle points to 75," I directed. "That's WSB. It's probably the only station you can get clear." I know a lot about radios. We never have owned one, but Nutty's grandpa has one and I've listened to it several times. Also, my teacher last year believed in such things and brought one to school whenever the President or the Governor or anybody important made a speech.

Clara May twisted the right-hand knob again. "It doesn't have any static at all, does it?" she said proudly. Most radios do sputter, but this one was as quiet as could be.

"Here," I said, "let me try it," and she moved away for me to see if I could locate WSB or any other station that might be heard. I set the needle on 75 exactly and then turned up the sound control knob as high as it would go. I expected it to suddenly blast away, but nothing happened.

Skinny Little Renfroe said, "It sure don't have any static whatsoever."

I lifted up the radio to look behind it and saw that there was a cord and plug attached to it. "What's the matter with you two?" I asked, trying to sound as provoked as I was. "This-here is an electric one."

"Not *this-here*," said Clara May. "*This* will suffice."

Skinny Little Renfroe said, "Why, it can't be! We don't have electricity, D. J., you know that."

Now if they weren't both as crazy as coots, I don't know what is! Here they hadn't had sense enough to order a battery radio, and when I pointed out the trouble to them, Clara May stopped to give me an English lesson while Skinny Little Renfroe let me in on the big news that we didn't have electricity at our house.

He rattled on now as if he were certain everything would be all right if he could just convince me of it. He said, "Those mail-order folks wouldn't have sent us an electric one. They'd know what kind we needed."

"They'd send you the kind you ordered," I said.

"But just town folks have electricity."

"Yes," I answered, "and just town folks have electric radios."

He probably wouldn't be convinced of it yet if Clara May hadn't finally decided that she had made a mistake. "I guess I ordered the wrong kind," she admitted, her voice becoming sort of high-pitched and quavery.

Skinny Little Renfroe's face looked as if he'd been kicked in it. "But you can read!" he told her. It was a sore spot with him that he could not. "Didn't the catalogue say what sort it was?"

She answered, "I guess it must have, but I didn't realize there were two kinds. I don't know much about motors and things."

I laughed out loud. "A radio don't have no motor."

She didn't correct that sentence, and it with two mistakes in it, so I knew she was genuinely upset in spite of herself. She asked me, "Do you suppose we could buy us a battery for it?"

I began telling her how it took a different kind of radio altogether to operate on a battery, but before I was able to say much somebody called from the yard.

I went out to see who it was, and there stood every one of those Castor children—Doris and all four boys and even the two baby sisters, who were riding on Britt's and Monroe's shoulders.

"We came to visit Renfroe," said Chester, holding up a package. "Ma made him a blackberry pie."

"And I made him some tea cakes," said Doris, waving a paper sack at me.

Hoot said, "We also came to see the radio."

I could have fallen over. It's a well-known fact that news travels fast around here. It always has. But I was plumb stumped that a radio at our house had just been unwrapped and all of a sudden a yardful of neighbors from a mile up the road were saying they had come to see it.

Chester explained, "I ran into Clara May at the mailboxes." The Castors get their mail at the same junction we do.

Doris said, "She sent word for us to come see it."

That's just like Clara May! It wouldn't have surprised me if she had said for them to come and stay for supper. There's no telling what she'll do.

"The radio doesn't work," I said, and every one of them groaned.

"We were coming to see Renfroe, anyway," said Doris. "Aren't you mannerly enough to invite us in?"

"Go on in," I said, and they went scurrying up on

the porch and into the house like a drove of tame chickens.

After they got through admiring the radio, Britt allowed it was a pity that we couldn't use it. "Just think," he said, "if it would work we could turn on one of those knobs and quick-as-a-wink have us some entertainment."

At that, I thought Skinny Little Renfroe was going to spring out of the bed. He sat up quickly and stuffed the pillow back of him. "Entertainment?" he said. "Why, everybody just have a seat now! Everybody just sit down!"

The way those Castors obeyed him you'd have thought he was some big general and they were the foot soldiers. They settled in chairs or onto the floor at once and he gazed around the room and announced: "An imitation. By Renfroe Madison."

9

HIRING DAY

Nutty got to our house the next day before we had finished breakfast, and I hopped up from the table.

Pa said, "You'll have to wait for Clara May."

"If she's big enough to pack peaches," I said, "she's big enough to walk two and a half miles to the packing shed by herself."

Clara May patted her lips with the corner of her napkin as if we had all day and said, "I was big enough to pack peaches last year too."

That was her way of reminding me that I hadn't been. Last year I had helped keep the hopper filled, but maybe this time I'd get a packing job.

Clara May had been one of the ringers, which is a good thing to be at the packing shed. Ringers select the choice peaches and pack them into neat rings and then use them as the top layer in the baskets. In the rest of each basket, good peaches are used too. But they aren't packed, the way the ones in the rings are, to show off their pretty side when the baskets are opened.

For some reason, Clara May turned out to have a special talent for ringing and last year packed more peaches than 'most anybody. Ringers get paid according to how much they do. They put one of their packer's tickets on each basket that they finish and somebody counts them later for pay purposes. The ticket-system helps the inspector too. On any basket that's packed wrong, he knows which ringer must do the work over.

The grown men nearly all work out in the orchards, gathering the peaches and bringing them to the shed. The rest of us work at one job or another in the packing procedure. Folks around here refer to the jobs in the orchard and at the shed as "working in the peaches." All except Clara May. She speaks of the "peach harvest." Leave it to her to put on airs.

Peach season comes along at a good time. It's late enough in the summer that unless it's been an unusually rainy year we're "out of the grass" with our crops and have time for spare jobs. And it's nice to earn extra money.

Skinny Little Renfroe had set his mind a month ago that this year he would qualify for one of the jobs at the shed too. He thought he was big enough to put labels on the baskets for the inspector, and I suppose he was right. Anybody can do that. But Dr. Coe had said, "No indeed!" when the subject had been mentioned to him.

Skinny Little Renfroe's pride appeared to be hurting worse than his foot when we started out that morning without him. He called to us, "Tell Mr. Parker Gray that I'll be there by Monday. He can count on me to put the labels on for him."

"You just get well," answered Clara May cheerily. "And don't let me forget to sit down tonight and write those mail-order folks a letter. Maybe they'll let us trade the radio in on something else. You be thinking about what we can buy." Pa had convinced them that their supply of money would not get a battery radio powerful enough to pick up any stations clearly.

At the junction by the mailboxes, we saw the Castors' wagon coming along the road and Clara May suggested we wait there.

"You wait," I said. "They're too slow for me and Nutty. We got more to do than just poke along."

So she perched herself on the bank back of the mail-boxes to wait. It would have tickled me good if they hadn't had room for her, but it turned out that they had hitched up their two-horse wagon and there was more than enough space. They invited me and Nutty to get in when they overtook us. "Hop on," called Mr. Castor. "Save your strength for next week. You'll need it to work in the peaches."

I half-expected Clara May to say, "You mean for the peach harvest, Mr. Castor," but she didn't.

We scrambled onto the wagon and the whip was cracked overhead to get the mules in a faster-moving notion. The Castors wanted to hear how Skinny Little Renfroe was doing, so Clara May reported on him. Then we got started talking about jobs at the packing shed.

Hoot said, "I'm hoping to work at the hopper this year."

I was about to tell him he wasn't big enough when Britt said, "No, Hoot, I expect you'll handle the labels. Chester and I will probably feed the hopper." By that, he meant they would dump the peaches that came in from the orchard into the big hopper at the shed. That was the first step in the packing process.

I said, "Those jobs always go to me and Nutty."

Chester spoke up. "Not this year. I figure you're both big enough to be ringers."

Of course, I couldn't get mad with him for saying that, because down deep I was hoping that's what I'd be called on to do. Then he added, in all seriousness, "Unless Mr. Parker Gray thinks I've filled out enough to handle a packing bin myself."

Everybody laughed because it was far-fetched enough to think that Nutty and I, and maybe Monroe, might get to pack. Chester was plumb out of his mind for even dreaming that he was big enough. But Chester is generally out of his mind, anyway, and as we rode along he continued to juggle around the job possibilities. "Maybe I'll be asked to handle the culls," he said.

"That would be a good job for you," I said. "Selling rotten peaches to town folks!" Of course, that wasn't a fair thing for me to say. Most culls are perfectly good, but they're too ripe to hold up in shipping, or they have small defects of one kind or another, and are sold cheap to folks around here—farm or town people.

Chester didn't pay any attention to my comment, but went right on organizing. "Only if I handle the culls," he said, "somebody else will have to help Britt at the hopper. Nutty, why don't you do that?" You'd have thought he was Mr. Parker Gray himself. But because he continued to think I should be a ringer, I didn't get aggravated with him or any of the others. Even Doris didn't get on my nerves, but that may be because she and Clara May sat near the front and had begun a conversation of their own. But she hadn't irritated me even before that. Maybe peach season brings out the good in girls.

We were the seventh wagon to tie up at the packing shed, and there were people milling around all over. Some of them had come by foot. The grownups appeared not to have seen each other recently and were busy catching up on the news. The younger ones of us boys went out beyond the horse trough and chose sides to play a game of ball. A ball and bat and a few old gloves are kept at the shed, kindness of Mr. Gray. He says they keep boys out of devilment when the work is caught up.

We had only played one inning—and my side was up to bat again—when Mr. Gray came onto the loading platform of the shed. He was followed by Mr. Al Gibbons, his brother-in-law who helps run the farm and orchard. Our ball game ended then and we gathered around with everybody else to offer our services for the coming weeks.

Mr. Gray looked at me and asked, "Your Pa not here?"

"No, sir," I answered, "but he sent word that he could help. He's finishing up some work at home so he'll be in the clear by next week."

"Good," said Mr. Gray. "I want him to head-up one crew. Tell him to meet us over at the center orchard Monday morning. We'll begin on the Early Roses, same as always." Early Rose is the peach variety that ripens first around here. We call it the pickling peach because that's mainly what it's used for.

Mr. Gray then began making arrangements with the other men who were to gather the peaches, while Mr. Gibbons got out a pad and jotted down their names. Also, men were given the heaviest jobs at the shed and loading platform. At last, Mr. Gray began to select the packers, or ringers, whichever you want to call them. It gets to be confusing, because every job has something to do with packing—whether it's the actual packing or the sorting or stamping or what.

"Clara May Madison," said Mr. Gray, "you're to pack, for sure."

Mrs. Otis Conway called out, "She's a good 'un!" and Mr. Gray agreed: "Best we've ever had!" I could see that flattery going to Clara May's head.

Charlie Brand said, "But I'll beat her this time. Just wait!"

Everbody laughed and Mr. Gray said, "All right, Charlie, we'll count on you to be a ringer too. And let's see, who else?" He looked around and began to name different ones of the women and some of the older boys and girls. Then he picked Monroe Castor. I don't know why he picked him over me and Nutty.

99

We could handle any responsibility he could, but he was wearing an old straw hat and his shirt was on top of his overalls instead of tucked in, and maybe he looked nearer grown.

Mr. Gray took the list Mr. Gibbons had been making and counted down the page. "Seems we need one more ringer," he said, glancing around. Then he looked straight at me. "D. J., suppose you give it a try. And if you decide you don't like it, we'll give Nutty a chance." By that, he meant that if I didn't turn out to be any good at it, I would be replaced.

Then he named Nutty and Britt to keep the hopper filled, and Doris was to be one of the sorters. Chester, sure enough, impressed Mr. Gray that he was big enough to sell culls to visitors who might care to buy them.

The rest of the odd jobs were assigned next, with almost everybody being considered for one thing or another—or everybody except Ratty Logan. This is the first year he ever showed up looking for a job and Mr. Gray says it may as well be the last one. He says he's not about to take on as a worker anybody who's noted for getting into fights. It caused me to think twice about my inclination toward squabbling.

The last job called out was the one for putting labels on the baskets and it went to Hoot Castor. After that, Mr. Gray and Mr. Gibbons thanked the crowd for coming out and said they would see us Monday. Pickers and haulers were to begin early in the morning. They naturally had to get a head-start before the rest of us would have anything to pack. We were to show up by midmorning.

The only real aggravation to me about the whole commotion of hiring day was that the job assignments turned out to be exactly as Chester Castor had predicted them. And don't think he didn't brag about it all the way home. Next year he'd probably be put in charge of the hiring and firing, from the way he talked.

Dr. Coe was at the house when we got there. He had already examined Skinny Little Renfroe's foot and he and Mamma and Pa were talking in low tones in the kitchen. I caught just a few words, something about "serious infection," as I went past them into the bedroom.

Skinny Little Renfroe asked, "Did you tell 'em?"

"Tell who what?"

"Did you tell 'em at the packing shed that I want to put labels on the baskets for the inspector?"

I said, "Hoot Castor got that job."

"Then I can do something else. What other jobs are there?"

"Listen," I said, "even if your foot wasn't hurt, they wouldn't hire anybody five years old."

"I'm almost six," he said. "And besides, they hired Hoot."

"But he's eight—more than two years older than

you—and will be in the third grade when school starts."

Skinny Little Renfroe looked indignant. "I can say the alphabet," he said, as if that settled everything. Before I could reply, the doctor and Mamma came into the room.

"Renfroe," said Dr. Coe, "I want to get some of those Atlanta doctors to see if they can help us get your foot well."

"We don't know any Atlanta doctors," said Skinny Little Renfroe. "Do we, Mamma?"

The doctor smiled. "I know a few of them. But we'll have to take you up there to a hospital so they can watch after you."

I suppose they were expecting him to object, because Mamma started right in talking. "I'll go up with you," she said, "and stay close by for the first few days." She sort of bit her lip, like she hadn't planned to let on that he would have to stay more than a day or two.

Folks around here have to be mighty sick before any mention of hospitals is made. Clara May and I knew it and we appeared more worried than Skinny Little Renfroe, who seemed to be thinking about something else. He turned to Dr. Coe and said, "I don't suppose we'll go in your car?"

"Of course we will," replied Dr. Coe, and Skinny Little Renfroe was still grinning half an hour later when Pa lifted him out to the automobile.

IO

"IN THE PEACHES"

It puzzles some folks as to how the top layer or face of a basket of peaches can be packed before the bottom one. It amounts to doing the whole thing upside down. Metal forms are used that are taken away later when baskets are slid over them.

Ringers work with a round pan-looking thing called a facing form. The peaches have to be packed into it in nice tight rings. Next, a metal shell is fastened onto this. The shell looks like a basket with no top or bottom until it's put onto the facing form, when the two combined look a little like a basket turned wrong side up. After the rings are carefully packed and the shell has been attached, peaches from the bin are run gently into the whole thing.

Men usually take over for the next step. The forms have to be shaken down to get the fruit settled, and when completely full, are taken to benches where a basket is fitted over them. There they are flipped right side up for the first time. The facing form is then removed and the metal shell is pulled out, leaving only a basket of peaches ready to have the lid attached.

The first week I had to rework a lot of the baskets I packed. Either the rings weren't tight enough and had not passed inspection, or else I had included a peach that should not have been used. The sorters are supposed to not let any culls get to the packers, but, of course, nobody is absolutely perfect. But that didn't keep me from blaming Doris Castor whenever it appeared that a sorter had made a mistake. Monroe worked at the packing bin next to mine, and whenever we saw a bad peach we'd say, "A present from Doris."

I teased her about it one afternoon in the wagon on the way home. She said, "Why sure, I send along a rotten peach every now and then to let you know what I think of you."

I should have left it at that, but my answer was: "Is that what it signifies? Well, well! And just think of all the good ones you send me too." For some reason, it sounded more like a valentine than anything else. Her face turned reddish and I felt a little embarrassed myself.

Clara May spoke up. "What I want to know, Doris, is who supplies Mrs. Freddy Whitt with her bad ones?"

We all laughed then and got started talking about Mrs. Freddy Whitt. She's the worst ringer there ever was. She has to rework at least half her baskets because they're seldom done right the first time. Besides ringing too slack, she somehow can't tell a sorry peach from a choice one. Mr. Luther Brinson, the inspector, says that if there weren't but one peach in the world with a worm hole in it, Mrs. Freddy Whitt would find it and put it smack on the top in one of her baskets.

Once somebody had sneaked into the shed at lunch time and poured a basketful of culls into her bin. And in the afternoon, she used them as top peaches until the joke was discovered by Mr. Brinson. He'd like to fire her, I'm sure, except she's Mr. Parker Gray's wife's cousin.

In spite of being a ringer and making more money than I ever had, working at the shed was not the fun it once was. The weather seemed hotter, the peach fuzz seemed fuzzier and stickier, and the days seemed longer. Monroe Castor said it was the same as always to him. "Maybe it seems different to you because you're worried about Renfroe off up yonder in Atlanta," he said.

"Maybe that's it," I answered, admitting to myself that of course that was exactly what was the matter. It didn't seem right for Skinny Little Renfroe not to be home. As much as I fussed about the noise he made and him tagging along after me, and things like that, it wasn't a good feeling for him not to be around. And something inside me kept saying, *Yeah, and it's all your fault.*

Monroe asked, "When can he come home?"

"We don't know yet," I said, just as a fresh batch of peaches came down the belt and we stopped talking and went back to work.

Mamma had stayed with Skinny Little Renfroe the first week, and part of the second one, but she had to come home then to see about us and to get some clean clothes.

The day she was going back was payday for Clara May and me. We decided to buy something to send Skinny Little Renfroe and went at lunch time to the store at the crossroads. But we'd have to make our purchases in a hurry if we were to get them out to the main road to Mamma. She would be waiting there to catch the mail bus to town, where she could catch a train on to Atlanta.

The store at the crossroads sells groceries, and work clothes, and yardgoods, and hardware—nails, plow points, and things like that. It also sells seed and fertilizer. In fact, it sells almost everything that's absolutely necessary for day-to-day living, but not a whole lot that might cheer up a boy who was off sick in a hospital. Mamma was taking candy and bananas, and we tried to think of something else.

"I know what I'll send him," said Clara May. "Fig Newtons." And she reached across the counter and picked up a box of them.

"That's a good idea," I said, and took a box too. I expected her to call me a copycat and say I ought to think up something of my own. But she said, "I'll bet there's not anything he'd rather have than two boxes of Fig Newtons." Then she added, "Maybe we ought to send him something to drink with them."

"How about some belly washers?" I suggested.

She stiffened, the way she does when my language happens not to suit her. "Are you referring to King Mountain Colas?" she asked.

"Yes," I said, imitating her prissy voice, "I was referring to King Mountain Colas."

She switched to sounding natural again and said, "That's a splendid idea. Let's buy him three apiece."

We paid Mr. Ollie, the storekeeper, for our purchases a few minutes later and hurried out to the main road, but our folks weren't there. "Maybe they've come and gone," I said.

"No," said Clara May. "We'd have met Pa on his way back to the orchards." He had gotten off to fetch Mamma to where she could flag down the mail bus. Clara May continued, "But we don't have to wait for them. We can just leave our packages here. Mamma'll know they're from us to Renfroe."

"Somebody might come along and take them."

"Only mean children would do a thing like that," she said, steadying the bag against a rock by the side of the road. "And all the mean children around here are busy packing peaches. Come on, or we'll be late."

Just then we heard a wagon rattling along the road, and a minute later Mamma and Pa drove up. We showed them our presents and Mamma said she had room in her suitcase for the Fig Newtons, but the drinks would take up too much space. Besides, they might weight her down. She would have a long walk in Atlanta from the station to the hospital.

So we took the King Mountain Colas back to the packing shed, discussing on the way who we might share them with.

Nutty could have one of mine. And I hated to admit it, but after working next to Monroe Castor all this time I had begun to get along with him. Maybe I'd give him one of the drinks.

Clara May said, "I'm not particular about who shares mine, just so it's not Charlie."

She was talking about Charlie Brand, her strongest rival in ringing peaches. "You're jealous of him," I said.

She snapped, "I am not. He's just stuck-up, that's all." I didn't say anything, and she added, "He's stuck-up because he's so handsome."

She had said more than she meant to, I could tell. I laughed. "Who said he was all that handsome?"

"Nobody said it," she answered. "But he thinks it, I'll bet."

"If he's stuck-up, it's because he's the best peach-packer."

"He is not," she said flatly. "He was ahead of me last week, but I'm gaining on him now. I'll probably beat him for the season."

"No, you won't," I predicted. And when we got back to the shed, I aggravated her further. "Look over there," I said. "I reckon the other girls think Charlie is as handsome as you do." Two or three of them were standing back of him, trying to get his attention while he went on with his work.

Actually, Charlie is a good sport. I don't imagine he relishes it when some girl like Clara May can do as good a job as he can, but who blames him for that? When the work is caught up and we have time for a game of ball, he's one of the best players there is. And he don't ever push around me and Nutty and the Castors the way some of the bigger boys try to. I'd say that Charlie Brand is well-liked by 'most everybody—or everybody except Clara May.

The machinery was running and I hurried over to my bin. Nobody said anything to me about being late. Since we get paid according to the number of baskets we do, it's to our own advantage to always be there.

Middle of that afternoon, the distributing belt broke down and the work came to a standstill. Mr. Buck Jordan, the official mechanic, set about repairing it, and the rest of us went outside. The grown folks sat out under the trees and talked, and the others went different directions. Some of the packers went out to the well and drew a fresh bucket of water.

Clara May and I gathered up some of our friends and went out and sat on the shady side of the loading platform while we drank the King Mountain Colas. We had more friends than we did drinks, but King Mountains are whopper-size, and we passed the bottles around and let everybody have a sip or two. Clara May says it's not sanitary to do that, but she doesn't like hurting anybody's feelings and wouldn't let on that there wasn't gracious plenty to go around. In fact, she was so hospitable in seeing that everybody got a few swallows, I'm not sure she got any herself. That shows how dumb she is. She was saying, "Now, Hoot, you must have another taste," looking after him, I guess, because he was the littlest one there, when Charlie strolled over. I thought surely that would cause her to stop acting as if she were a noble princess throwing a royal barbecue. From the way she pretended to dislike him, it would seem that she'd have threatened to hit him in the head with one of the bottles if he didn't get on out of the way.

But she smiled at him as if he were one of her dearest friends. She's a downright hypocrite. "Would you care to share our drinks with us?" she asked. "Britt, is there another swallow in the one you've got?"

Britt, of course, handed the bottle to Charlie, who said, "Thank you kindly," and turned it up for a swig. "Thank you again," he said, when he put it down. He started to sit with us, but Mr. Brinson motioned for everybody to come back inside. The belt had been repaired.

An hour later the machinery rumbled to a halt again, and I figured the belt must not have been patched up too good. But Mr. Al Gibbons came out of his wire-enclosed office up front and reported to us that we were switching varieties. "These are the last of the Georgia Belles," he said, motioning toward the peaches that were in the bins. "Get 'em packed and out of the way, and we'll get started on the Elbertas. There are two wagons of 'em waiting outside now."

Everybody was excited as we cleaned out the bins. The Elberta was the last variety to ripen and also the most important of all. More orchard space was given over to it than any other kind. It doesn't taste all that much better than the rest, but it's what Mr. Parker Gray calls *a good shipper*. By that, he means it doesn't get bruised up like some of the thinner-skinned ones and can be shipped to far-off places easier. We all knew that once Elbertas ripened, we were in for a week or more of steady work from daylight till dark—and then the season would be over.

When the Georgia Belles were cleared out, the machinery was cranked up again. Soon the big belt was supplying the bins with the new variety—and the rush was on.

At home two nights later, we had a letter from Mamma. Pa and Clara May and I decided from it that Skinny Little Renfroe must be getting well. What Mamma had actually said was that his condition did not appear to be worse, and we told ourselves that he must therefore be better. That was what we wanted to believe. We held out against admitting that it was a bad sign for him not to be showing improvement by now.

I began then to believe everything would surely turn out all right and concentrated more on peach-packing than anything else. I thought about Skinny Little Renfroe and wished he would come on home, but no notion that he might not get well ever crossed my mind.

The only thing that worried me during the final days of the season was that Clara May might turn out to have packed more than anybody else. She and Charlie were almost even by now. Mrs. Estella Ray had done more than either one of them at one point, but she fell behind when she had to be out a whole day.

I knew how bad it would be on me if Clara May did come out ahead. Since I was a ringer this year, too, she wouldn't let any opportunity go by to remind me of how skilled she had been—and that I hadn't set any record. Even so, I hadn't planned to do anything underhanded to keep her from winning. I'd be the first to admit I was hoping she wouldn't, but I didn't meditate over any scheme to keep her from it. But when the chance presented itself, I took it. I regretted what I did almost immediately, but by then it was too late.

I I

THE HURT TO CLARA MAY

Clara May makes biscuits the same way Mamma does,
by pouring milk into a wooden bowl filled with flour.
The milk makes a little puddle at first, but gradually
flour is mixed into it until it becomes dough. Somewhere along the line baking powder and salt are supposed to be added, but Clara May generally forgets
one or the other of those, sometimes both. But her
main trouble is that she never can gauge how much to
make. One day we'll have a plateful of biscuits left

over, and the next time there are barely enough to go around.

That's what had happened at breakfast on the day I caused the hurt to her. Actually, we had plenty of biscuits to eat that morning, and one or two for Andrew Jackson, but there weren't enough extra ones for three lunches. Pa said, "That's all right. We'll celebrate this being the last day of the peach season by buying our lunch." At that, he reached across the table and picked up the plate of fatback. "That allows us to finish this, too," he said, and we divided the meat that had been held back for the lunches.

At noon, Clara May and I left the packing shed and went over to the store at the crossroads. Pa had given us some of his money to spend, along with instructions on what to buy, so there was nothing to argue about inside the store. We bought three cans of sardines, a wedge of cheese, and a box of soda crackers.

"Why don't you take Pa his lunch?" I said, when we were outside.

"'Cause he said for you to," answered Clara May, and I knew there was no way out of it. She stopped and divided the cheese into three pieces and the crackers into even amounts. Then she started back to the packing shed and I set out to the fartherest orchard where Pa and his crew were gathering the last of the Elbertas.

They weren't ready to break for lunch when I got

there and I put Pa's lunch in the fork of one of the trees for him and headed back to the packing shed. I stopped along the path to open my can of sardines, then hurried on, eating as I went.

The gong had not sounded for the crowd to get back to work and it appeared that everybody was on the other side of the shed, either playing ball or watching the game. I took a shortcut through the shed to get to the game quicker.

I was mad that I hadn't gotten to play. And it was all Clara May's fault. She was probably out cheering one of the teams, while I had missed the fun purely because she hadn't had sense enough to make the right amount of biscuit dough. That's what I was thinking about when I stopped suddenly at the lidding benches. I looked around and nobody was in sight. It was a funny feeling to be in the shed when everything was quiet.

Baskets, completely packed but with no lids on them yet, were left on the long benches and the packer's tickets in each one were signs that they had not been inspected. It came to me that I could do something to slow down Clara May during the afternoon. Then maybe she wouldn't be champion packer for the summer and I wouldn't have to listen to her brag about it all year. My first thought was to put a few knotty peaches in the top of her baskets. Then the inspector would send them back and she would have to stop to do them over. But I didn't see any culls handy and it struck me that I could just switch some packer's tickets instead.

Mrs. Freddy Whitt's baskets were all the time having to be done over. There's no telling what her percentage of turned-down baskets actually was, but it kept one man busy trotting back and forth with work for her to do again.

So I traded packer's tickets on half-a-dozen of her baskets with the same number of Clara May's. That way, the rejected ones would go back to Clara May to be done over.

After I did it, I sneaked on toward the front of the shed, but before I got there I had a sick feeling inside me. I stopped a second and was on the verge of going back to make amends. But the gong sounded and the crowd started back into the shed.

I was feeling plumb disgusted with myself by the time work got underway. I felt even worse, not long afterwards, when I saw four baskets being taken to Clara May to be repacked. Apparently the other two of Mrs. Whitt's had passed inspection.

Clara May looked as if something had hit her. She couldn't seem to believe she had packed four unsatisfactory baskets, but her tickets were there for proof.

Mr. Luther Brinson, the inspector, said, "Maybe

you're trying to go a little too fast here on the last day," and of course Clara May had to stop and repack every one of them.

After they were finished, she seemed to slow down on her regular packing. I guess she didn't want to risk having any more baskets turned down. A troubled expression was on her face, and I tried not to look at her. Bending over my own bin, I concentrated so hard on what I was doing that I barely heard Monroe saying that the last load of Elbertas was being unloaded. We would be finished long before dark.

A few minutes later Pa came along to tell Clara May and me that he and the picking crews had been paid off and he was going on home. That was around two-thirty, and by four o'clock, or a few minutes after, the packing was finished. The platform crew had to get the baskets cleared out, but the rest of us were called up front to collect our wages.

Mr. Parker Gray said, "Ladies and gentlemen, it's been a real good year. You've all worked hard and I'm proud of each and every one of you." He went on to make a speech, which was the same one he had made last year and the year before. At the end of it, he told us that he would throw his annual square dance at the shed as soon as the machinery had been cleaned and oiled and covered up for the winter. "And each man, woman, and child among you is invited," he said, and everybody acted surprised, as if we hadn't been counting on the square dance all the time. It was the way we always wound up the summer.

Then he said, "Your pay will be ready in a minute. It's being counted out by Brother Al." That's what he calls Mr. Al Gibbons, his brother-in-law. "And the top packer is going to get a bonus this time," he continued. "Brother Al and I decided to make it ten dollars."

Everybody began murmuring, speculating on whether Clara May or Charlie would win. Some thought Mrs. Estella Ray still might have a chance at it, but that wasn't likely since she'd been out a day. I didn't join in the discussion because all I could think about was what I'd done to Clara May. As hard as money was to come by, what if she had lost out on account of me?

Mr. Gibbons came out with our pay and the record slips. "Looks like Charlie gets the extra ten dollars," he said, handing out the first pay. "And Clara May, here's your wages. You just barely missed the prize." Looking at the slip of paper with her money, he added, "You were only three baskets behind."

Mrs. Otis Conway patted Clara May on the back. "If you just hadn't run into rotten luck with the ones you had to do over!"

Charlie's supporters were saying they'd known all the time that he would win, and while the rest of us were being paid, I heard Clara May congratulating him herself. And he told her it would be his pleasure to treat her and me to a Coca-Cola, or whatever we wanted, at the store if we had time to stop off with him. But she said we would have to be going home.

We caught a ride with the Castors in their wagon and listened most of the way to Chester's views of how next year's packing would go and what jobs each one of us were apt to get. Clara May and I got off at the side road that led to our house, and Nutty and the Castors rode on. As soon as they were out of ear shot, Clara May stopped pretending to be such a cheerful loser. She said, "If I could have just beat Charlie! With Renfroe being in the hospital and all, we need money more than ever."

Without thinking, I said, "I didn't know about the ten-dollar bonus when I—"

She looked at me and I stopped. Then I blurted out, "I caused you to lose. I switched packer's tickets." I went on then and told her what I'd done. It didn't seem to come out sounding like I was genuinely as ashamed of myself as I was, but at least I explained what had happened. She listened without saying a word and when I finished, she still didn't speak. Finally, I stopped in the middle of the road. "I'm going back," I told her. "I'll confess the whole thing to Mr. Parker Gray. Then you'll get the money."

Clara May stopped and looked me square in the eyes for a few seconds, then said calmly, "He wouldn't believe you. And it would hurt Charlie now. Besides, everybody would think you made it up so we could get the money."

"Then I'll give you ten dollars of my own," I said.

"I don't accept charity," she said, walking on ahead so fast that I had to run to keep up.

When we were nearly home, I nagged, "Tell Pa on me. See if I care!"

"I'm not going to tell on you."

"Then I'll tell," I said. "I'll tell him—and Mamma, too, when she comes home."

She stopped and glowered at me. "Don't you dare say a word to them."

"Why not?"

"Because they're upset too much already about Renfroe."

I said, "I'd feel better to tell it and get whipped for doing it and be done with it."

"You don't deserve to be done with it," she said. Staring at me coldly, she said, "I want you to promise me one thing: That you won't ever worry Mamma and Pa by telling them how low-down you've acted."

We were nearly home then and I said, "All right, if that's the way you want it."

"That's the way I want it," she said.

When we got nearly to our house we saw Dr. Coe's car in the back yard. "Maybe Renfroe is home," said Clara May and we started running.

We were met at the back door by Pa and I could tell

by his face that something was wrong. Also, he had
put on his Sunday clothes.

"Where you going?" I asked.

"The doctor came for me," he said. "He and I have
to go to Atlanta. The doctors up there are having to
make a decision about Renfroe's leg."

"He's gonna be all right," said Clara May, in a high-
pitched tone. "I'm sure he's going to be all right."

Neither one of us seemed to want to ask what sort
of decision was having to be made and Pa started in
telling us to take care of all the chores. "I've fed the
bull," he said. That was the one animal on the place
Pa looked after himself. He was going to turn him
over to me as soon as we could put a ring in his nose.
That would make him easier to manage. Pa continued,
"And go ahead and have your supper and don't wait
up for me. It may be the middle of the night or even
tomorrow before I get back."

By then, Dr. Coe had come out onto the porch, too,
and I asked Pa, "What sort of decision has got to be
made?"

Pa looked at the doctor, then back at us. "They may
have to amputate," he said.

Clara May screamed, "Don't let 'em cut his leg off!
Don't let 'em!" She sounded hysterical, and Dr. Coe
spoke up.

He said, "Now, now!" and came over and patted us
both on the back. "The infection has been complicated

by blood poisoning, and that's a *mighty* serious matter. The doctors there are going to do everything they can."

"To save his leg?" said Clara May, in a pleading tone.

"To save his life," answered Dr. Coe.

He and Pa left then, and Clara May went in the kitchen and flopped down on the covered woodbox that serves as a bench too. She leaned across it and cried like a bawling baby. I was sort of in a daze about everything myself and just stood in the middle of the floor.

At last, I took down the milking buckets from the pantry shelf. "I'll do the milking for you," I told her.

"I'll do it," she said, getting to her feet. "I'm all right now." And she went to the barn to do her part of the work while I set out to feed the hogs and see about the mules.

12

"A PART OF THE FAMILY"

Depending on the year—how dry or how wet it's been, how early or late we're running with the crops—we may have plenty of farm work to do as soon as peach season is over, or we may not have a whole lot for another few weeks. This year the work was pretty well caught up at the time and I decided to look for an in-between job. The notion struck me the night Pa and Dr. Coe went to Atlanta. I could earn extra money and try again to pay Clara May the ten dollars I'd kept her from winning. Of course I owed her more than money too.

Pa had still not gotten home by sunup the next day and Clara May and I got up on schedule and did the morning chores. After we had eaten breakfast I mentioned my plan about hiring out.

She thought it was a good idea and suggested I go back to the packing shed. "Maybe Mr. Buck Jordan needs somebody to help him clean the equipment."

"I'll try there first," I said. "And besides the money, I could learn a lot from Mr. Jordan. He's give up to be one of the best mechanics around here."

Clara May stopped pouring water from the kettle into the dishpan and looked at me.

"All right," I said, trying to beat her to the correction. "He's knowed as one of the best mechanics."

"*Known*," she said, as I set off to hunt a paying job while she got on with the housework.

The shed was empty except for Mr. Al Gibbons, who was inside the screened-in office going over some paper work. "We can probably use you," he said, after I had inquired. "Most of the young men hereabouts won't be worth killing until they get through spending the money they earned in the peaches." Then he sent me down to the wagon shelter and toolroom to talk to Mr. Buck Jordan.

When I found him he was under a wagon chassis and I squatted down and yelled up under it what I was doing there. "Sure," he called back, "I can use you." A minute later he pushed himself out from under the wagon and stood up. "If Al Gibbons is willing to pay you, I'm willing to have you," he said. "It'll be handy to have an assistant." He selected a screwdriver from a toolbox. "As a matter of fact, I may just teach you to do the work and I'll sit back and supervise. How about it?"

"Fine," I said, hoping he would let me do a lot of different things.

"Before we start on the packing house equipment," he said, "I've got to get this brace fastened to the axle." Grinning, he asked, "Can you help me with it, or do you specialize altogether in peach machinery?" Without waiting for an answer, he crawled under the wagon again. "Now if you'll hand me that Stillson wrench over there, our partnership will be off to a good start."

I picked up a tool that was near my feet and held it under the wagon to him. "That's a socket wrench," he said. "The Stillson is the big one there in the corner."

I was expecting him to make a joke about my not knowing the difference, but instead he explained the uses for each wrench while he went ahead with the work. Every now and then he would call for something else, and I was glad to stay busy. It kept my mind off what might have happened at the hospital.

"A Part of the Family"

By noon, I had gotten used to where most of the tools were kept and had even had a chance to use one or two of them. When we stopped work, I explained to Mr. Jordan, "I didn't know I would be hired so readily and I came off down here without my lunch. If you wouldn't mind, I expect I'd better go home and eat, but I'll hurry back."

"Why, you needn't do that," he said. "I have one sandwich more than I need. And I'll buy us a Coke apiece if you'll run down to the crossroads and fetch them." He handed me a quarter.

"I couldn't cause you to have to divide your lunch," I said, as he sat down on an upturned keg near the doorway and began to unwrap his sandwiches.

"Ain't you back from the store yet?" he asked, in a way that I knew it was all settled. I ran to get the drinks.

In a way, I was glad not to be going home. Pa would surely be there by then and could tell me what sort of decision had been made. But in the event the news was bad, I had just as soon not hear it yet. I hated to face up to the fact that everything might not be all right—that Skinny Little Renfroe might be suffering something awful. And I couldn't put it out of my mind, the way I used to, that I caused him his trouble.

I knew that whatever had been necessary at the hospital would have already been decided and done. But at the same time I felt almost that until I had actually heard the news, chances of things turning out in our favor were continually getting better. It was a mixed-up feeling, and I was glad that Mr. Jordan and I got started on the packing equipment as soon as we finished eating. We were so busy all afternoon that I didn't have time for any extra thinking.

By the time I got home, I feared going into the house. Maybe I'd better go take the salt block out of the barn and put it at the edge of the pasture where Twilight and Effie could get at it. But when I started in that direction, Pa came across the yard. He said, "Clara May told me where you went. Did you get a job?"

"Yes, sir," I said. "I'm helping Mr. Jordan clean up the machinery. When did you get home?"

"Middle of the morning," he said. I looked at him, hesitating to ask more. "Renfroe's better," he said at last. "The doctors decided against operating for the time being. It may not be necessary after all."

At the end of the next week I got my first pay on the new job. Put together with what I had made in the peaches, it was more money than I had ever had. I tried to pay Clara May the ten dollars I caused her to lose out on, but she refused again. I asked her, "Are you gonna buy clothes with your peach money?"

"No," she said, "I'm gonna give it to Pa to help out on the hospital bill," and at supper she told him of her intention. Before I realized it, I had offered him my money too.

"No," he said, "you both need to get some duds for school." We usually buy clothes with whatever money we earn in the peaches.

"I don't need any," I said. "And besides, I ought to have to pay the hospital bill by myself." They both looked at me and I continued, "It's my fault that he's in the hospital. I hit him in the foot with an ear of corn, and that's what got the trouble started." I went on to tell the whole story.

They listened without interrupting me, and when I was finished, Pa looked up. "You ought not to have done it," he said, shaking his head slowly, "but you mustn't blame yourself for what came afterwards. We all have cuts and bruises from time to time and it's a shame that Renfroe had one that developed into something serious. It's hard for us to always understand how and why things happen."

Clara May didn't say anything for a little while, then she said to Pa, "If you'd take my money and D. J.'s, it would help on the bills."

"No," he said firmly. "The cotton crop might see us through. And if not, well, this won't be the first time I've had to borrow against the next year's profits."

He pushed his chair back from the table. "And you know," he added, "if Renfroe gets well, I won't feel that we are at all poor."

Clara May got up and started taking the dirty plates to the dishpan. "In my recent correspondence with the mail-order house," she said, which meant she got a letter back from them, "they sent me a credit check for the radio we couldn't use. Do you suppose, Pa, that my peach money added to it could buy a battery radio that would give all of us pleasure?"

"Why, it might," said Pa. "But you'll be needing clothes more."

I said, "Let me pay for the rest of a radio."

Clara May snapped, "It's not your project."

"Why, Clara May," said Pa. "Don't let's discourage him if he has finally decided that he wants to be a part of the family." He went on to tell her that there are times when there is generosity in accepting as well as in giving, and that she might at least consider using some of my money. Of course, he didn't know about the way I had cheated her out of winning the bonus.

Instead of her admitting she didn't want me to go in on the radio, she said, "He needs his money for clothes too. His overalls are plumb ragged and he's outgrown them besides."

"I can let the straps down," I said, not wanting to lose the argument now that I had taken a side. "They'll do very well for another year."

Pa laughed. "And besides," he said, talking to Clara May, "he's not a girl who's going to be in the ninth grade in the fall."

"Oh, all right," said Clara May, "but he's not going to pay any more on it than I do," and she got out the catalogue and we all picked out the model we would buy. Then she got down a pencil and paper and figured out exactly how much I could pay so as not to have a bigger investment in the purchase than she did. She wouldn't trust me not to suddenly decide I owned more than half of it and expect too strong a say in how it was to be used. I didn't have any intention of being tricky about it, but I guess she's got a right not to trust me entirely. I suppose it will take a while for me to win over anybody's confidence—if I do decide that I want to become a part of the family.

13
"CHOOSE YOUR PARTNER"

Mr. Buck Jordan told me the following Saturday that I'd been the best helper he had ever had. And Mr. Al Gibbons said I would be called back any time an assistant mechanic was needed. I thanked them both and accepted my final wages and started home.

It was a good feeling to have days ahead with nothing urgent to be done. Picking cotton was our next big job and a few bolls were already beginning to open, reminding us that more hard work was coming. In the meantime, I would be able to go fishing with Nutty, or maybe drop over to the Castors for a visit or two. But I forgot all about plans of that sort when I got back to the house and found Skinny Little Renfroe there. He called from the porch, before I'd even seen him, "Guess who's home!"

"Me," I answered.

"No, me," he said. "I'm back."

"We've missed you," I told him, and he followed me inside, beginning a tale about everything that had happened to him since he'd been gone.

He was still talking late that night. I leaned out of my bed and blew out the lamp. In the darkness, he was quiet for a few seconds, then said, "I'll still be here when I wake up. Ain't that splendid?"

"Yes, it is," I answered. "Now go to sleep."

When word got around that he was back, folks from up and down the road came trailing in to see him. It was like a camp meeting for several days, with all the coming and going—and everybody bringing along good things to eat: cakes and pies and candy and shelled pecans roasted with salt and butter.

He was able to get up and stir about during part of each day, but the doctor wanted him to also rest a lot. He chose to do that mainly when company was there. He would pile up in bed and look as weak as possible. Seeing him so lifeless, visitors would say "Poor Renfroe!" in a tone that almost guaranteed they would go straight home and cook up more good things to bring him. They wouldn't know that when they cleared out, he would race Clara May and me to the kitchen to sample whatever had been brought along this time.

Finally, he got tired of the act and would have stayed up all the time if Mamma hadn't made him spend the afternoons in bed. But Nutty and the Castors would come over and we'd all go inside and visit with him while he got on with his resting.

One day Chester Castor asked him if he could still croak like a frog after all the work they did on him at the hospital. There was a whole roomful of us sitting around that day and some of the others said they weren't as interested in the frog imitation as they were the goat one. Then somebody else mentioned another one.

Skinny Little Renfroe beamed, waiting to see how many of his numbers could be recalled. Then he said, "I'll do a new one for you."

Nutty said, "That's a good idea. Let's hear a new one."

"It's going to be an old man snoring in the hospital," explained Skinny Little Renfroe. "A nurse is trying to get him to wake up on account of it's time to take some medicine because the doctor said so, but he don't care what the doctor said and goes back to snoring again and if you'll listen you'll hear the siren of an ambulance outside that's bringing in somebody who's been in an automobile wreck but not hurt too bad after all."

He stopped, drew a deep breath, and announced: "An imitation. By Renfroe Madison," and I figured he was well. I might also have guessed that in the days to come we would be hearing more and more imitations based on his hospital experiences.

"Renfroe," I said one night, "I'm plumb tired of hearing that," when he had all but turned into an ambulance siren.

"I'm just practicing it," he said. "You don't have to listen." Then his eyes brightened and he grinned. "You didn't call me Skinny Little Renfroe."

"You ain't skinny any more," I said. Actually, he had gained a pound or two, but I'd made up my mind anyhow to call him by his rightful name.

"Well," he said cheerily, "just for that I'll be glad to stop imitating a siren if you're tired of hearing it."

"Thank you."

"I'll do my jay-bird number for you instead," he announced, which wasn't what I had in mind, but Clara May came in about that time and we all talked about the radio. It still hadn't come. And the funny thing was that neither Clara May nor Renfroe had gotten used to the idea of me being in on it with them. Sometimes they still referred to it as the *you-know-what*.

"The longer it takes to get here," I said, "the longer we'll have to look forward to it," which sounded more like something one of them would say. They agreed that it's better to be looking toward something nice in the future than to always have everything you want. Renfroe got so carried away with the idea that he suggested we might ought to write the mail-order house and tell them to hold up on sending the radio a while longer.

"Don't worry," said Clara May, "it won't come for another week or two." She added happily, "But something else is coming before then."

"From the mail-order house?" I asked.

"No, an event."

"Oh, the square dance."

"Tomorrow night!" she said, and whirled around the room, limbering up the slippers she had bought for the coming year.

We hadn't been sure that Renfroe would get to come along until Dr. Coe said it would do him good to get out. So Pa and I hitched up the wagon, hooked a lantern onto it, and our whole family headed for the square dance. Andrew Jackson was along, naturally. He's not one for letting the wagon leave without him, even if it is night. Nutty came over and went with us too. His grandparents don't care for square dances, but 'most everybody else enjoys them. And families from all over this end of the county go to the big one every year at the packing shed.

Mr. Parker Gray always hires first-rate fiddlers, and a crackerjack caller too. This time the caller got the dancing started exactly on time. After the fiddlers had tuned up, he sang out:

> "All right everybody,
> Here we go!
> Choose your partner,
> And don't be slow."

Mamma and Pa were among the first couples to the center of the floor. There was a lot of stirring around and getting organized, folks speaking to one another and inquiring about how they'd been getting along. Charlie Brand started toward us and I thought he was coming over to talk to Nutty and me. But he stopped when he came to Clara May and asked her, "Would you be my partner?"

"Thank you," she said, getting to her feet. "I'd be pleased." He led her out to where the caller was directing the dancers:

> "Join your hands
> And circle around,
> With your right foot up
> And your left foot down."

137

Smaller children were invited mostly to watch, or to dance around the edge and not get in anybody's way. Ones my size could dance with the grown folks, but I wasn't too confident about the steps and wasn't sure I'd dance at all.

Clara May knows all the steps fine. They say good peach-packers are good square-dancers and there might be something to it. Clara May and Charlie were so sure of their footwork that they were worth watching. Seeing them, I got in the notion of trying the next set myself.

I went over and asked Doris Castor if she would care to be my partner, just the way Charlie had asked Clara May. I expected her to answer the same way, but she said, "The floor's too splintery." She added quickly, "It's not that I wouldn't like to." Then she giggled, "I didn't think about anybody asking me to dance or I'd have worn my shoes."

I sort of laughed too. "I didn't think about the splinters either," I said, looking down at my own bare feet.

Mr. Clem Darby was sitting nearby and had overheard us. He said in a loud voice, "You're growing up. Yes, siree, you're growing up." Then he laughed loudly and continued, "I'll bet you'll both wear shoes next year. When you start hankering to choose partners for a square dance you're getting the urge to be grown."

I hadn't gotten the urge to do anything except dance, and the whole world wouldn't have had to know it if he hadn't spread the news. Nutty and Renfroe said my face was red when I came back to where they were sitting.

The call ending the next dance was:

> "Chicken in the bread pan
> Picking up dough,
> Grab your partner
> And home you go."

Mamma and Pa came over to see about us then, and Charlie brought back Clara May. Pa said, "Why don't we all have a soda?" He motioned toward a tub of cold drinks. "They're put there for refreshments."

Charlie said, "Yes, sir, that's a good thought," and he and Nutty went with Pa to fetch enough drinks for all of us.

While they were gone, Clara May whispered to me that Charlie had said he was sorry if it hurt her feelings that he beat her packing peaches.

"Want me to tell him he didn't beat you?" I asked.

"Don't be crazy," she said. "He might not want to dance with anybody who could do more work than he could." He walked up about that time and she smiled at him as if she probably wouldn't ever have strength enough to pack another peach.

After a while, Clara May and Charlie didn't come back and join the family between all of the dances, but milled around and talked to other couples. I thought maybe I'd be sent to tell Clara May to come back to our side of the shed. In fact, I started to suggest it but decided against it, surprising myself that I chose not to cause aggravation. It wasn't too bad a feeling.

The dance ended not long after that and Charlie asked Pa if he could see Clara May home.

"No," said Pa. "It's too late, and you're both too young to be turned loose without a chaperon." Charlie didn't seem to know what to say till Pa added, "But you can ride home with us if you'd like."

"Yes, sir," said Charlie, "that'll be fine. Thank you, sir," and he hurried to get his mule. He could tie it to the back of our wagon and then ride it to his house later.

We lit the lantern and began to settle into our places, all except Andrew Jackson, who had not stirred from his the whole evening. Pa and Mamma rode up front and Charlie and Clara May sat on a board that fitted across the side bodies about middle-way. Somehow Renfroe wedged himself between them and sat there as if he had reserved the space ahead of time.

Clara May suggested to him, "Maybe you'd have more room if you sat somewhere else."

"This is all right," he said happily. "I'm real comfortable."

Of course he didn't realize that Clara May and Charlie might like to sit side by side. But I realized it. If I'd been seeing Doris home and Hoot Castor had

perched himself between us, I wouldn't have liked it.
Maybe I ought to help Clara May out.

"Renfroe," I said, "why don't you come back here
and sit with me and Nutty?"

"Yeah," said Nutty, "why don't you?"

Renfroe replied, "I'll sit with you all next time," as
if he didn't want to disappoint Charlie and Clara May
by leaving them alone.

I baited him by saying, "I want to hear one of your
imitations."

He asked excitedly, "Which one?" but did not leave
his seat.

"A new one I've thought up for you," I said. "Come
on back here and let's work it out."

"Let's do," he said, getting to his feet.

I could tell, even by dim lantern light, how happy
Clara May looked when she turned around to help
Renfroe get settled beside us. And he was grinning
mightily as he and Nutty and I talked in low tones. I
suggested he imitate a square-dance caller if he didn't
think it would be too difficult.

"That's a fine idea," he whispered. "And in between
the calls I'll imitate fiddle music and shuffling feet,
too, and from time to time I'll make a noise like a
soda bottle being uncapped over by the ice tubs."

"We'll introduce you," I said, and he smiled
proudly. A good feeling came over me, as if all of a
sudden I were no longer my own worst enemy—or

anybody else's. Nutty rapped on a floor board to get everyone's attention, and I made the announcement: "An imitation. By Renfroe Madison." To myself, I added: *Whose brother, D. J., is now a part of the family.*